PARANORMAL COZY MYSTERY

April Curses & May Hearses

TRIXIE SILVERTALE

Sittin' On A Goldmine
Productions L.L.C.

Sittin' On A Goldmine Productions, L.L.C.

pr@sittinonagoldmine.co

www.sittinonagoldmine.co

ISBN: 978-1-952739-65-1

Cover Design © Sittin' On A Goldmine Productions, L.L.C.

Cover design by Melony Paradise of Paradise Cover Design

Trixie Silvertale
April Curses and May Hearses: Paranormal Cozy Mystery : a novel / by Trixie Silvertale — 1st ed.
[1. Paranormal Cozy Mystery — Fiction. 2. Cozy Mystery —

Fiction. 3. Amateur Sleuths — Fiction. 4. Private Investigator — Fiction. 5. Wit and Humor — Fiction.] 1. Title.

CHAPTER 1

WINTER REFUSES to loosen its icy grip on Pin Cherry Harbor. My blowout twenty-sixth birthday bash had to be canceled due to a blizzard. Grams was distraught. I couldn't have been happier.

Instead of pasting on a smile for heaven knows how many hours, I was able to snuggle in front of my cozy fireplace while eating most of the dark chocolate with white-chocolate-raspberry ganache birthday cake my wonderful husband made for me. But that was back in March, on the first day of what passes for spring at this latitude.

Now, we're nearing the end of April, and the great lake nestled in the harbor behind my three-story bookshop is still locked in ice and snow.

The locals are eager for this elusive spring to reveal itself. I'd settle for a day with temperatures above freezing, or a sun that shares actual warmth, or — call me crazy — melting snow.

"Moon, are you coming into the office today?" My early-bird husband is up, dressed, and ready for action.

I make absolutely no effort to stifle my groan as I drag myself from the comfort of our cozy king bed.

"Yeah. I'm over halfway to getting my necessary private investigator hours. Why quit now?"

"You're a living saint." Erick laughs openly and blows me a kiss.

Throwing my hands in the air, I shuffle into the bathroom, splash some cold water on my face, and drag a brush through my haystack of snow-white hair.

"I'll be down in a minute. Don't leave without me."

"10-4. I'll have a pot of coffee ready for you. I'm leaving in five."

Former Sheriff Erick Harper is turning into quite an amazing husband. It took me years to convince myself that marriage was for me. However, now that I'm in it, I couldn't be happier.

Obviously, we don't agree on everything. Who does? But Erick learned a great deal about negotiation during his years as sheriff of Birch County. Comes in handy when you're married to a staunchly independent gal, such as myself.

Because of life-threatening temperatures out-side my snuggly walkup, I use the infamous layering technique while selecting today's wardrobe. Something I knew very little about before landing in almost-Canada.

Beginning with silk long underwear, I tuck those into wool socks, cover all of that with a pair of my beloved skinny jeans, and then throw three layers on my top half. My snarky T-shirts will have to wait for warmer weather. Maybe I could send Grams and Pyewacket on an online shopping mission? Somebody probably makes snarky sweaters, right? No. Best not to encourage the destructive duo.

By the time I seize the day and tromp down the stairs to the first floor of the three-story home I share with Erick, he is long gone. However, he left a sweet note on the counter. A large heart shape, and inside, he's drawn "E. H. + M. M."

What an adorable dork.

Before dragging myself to the PI office, I take my coffee for a walk and head over to the apartment to see if Ghost-ma or Pye have any helpful ideas.

The secret bookcase door slides open. As I step into my old apartment, I search high and low. "Grams? Grams, where are you?"

Multiple sparkles materialize to my left, and a

small ball of light swirls toward me, eventually taking the shape of Myrtle Isadora.

The additional wedding ring on her left hand reminds me of how close we came to losing her. As does the torn hem of her burgundy silk-and-tulle Marchesa gown and her missing silver Valentino.

"Thanks for using the slow, sparkly reentry method, Grams."

She casually twists one of her many strands of pearls and smirks. "Remember how terrified you used to get when I popped in out of nowhere? I was almost certain you might lose control of your bladder a couple of times."

"Hilarious. I do remember, and I can't say I ever cared for it. I'm much happier with this arrangement." Taking a seat on the plump settee, I lean back and sip my wake-up juice.

"Of course, dear. What's on the agenda?"

"Just have to put in my time at the agency. Can't let Erick be the only licensed detective."

"Competition can be healthy, but you do need to watch yourself, sweetie. Erick has far more experience than you. You could learn a lot from him."

Oh brother. "I'm well aware that you're Team Erick, Grams. There's no need for you to shake your pom-poms at this hour. I'm not in a competition with Erick. I'm only trying to pull my weight — as a valued member of the team."

My corporate-speak sends us both into a fit of giggles.

Ghost-ma is the first to calm herself. "Have you picked out a new ring?"

"New ring?"

She wiggles her ethereal left hand in my face a second time. "Yes, a new ring! Since you had to sacrifice yours to keep me on this side of the veil, I thought you would be excited to pick out a new one."

My brows knit together.

"What's the matter, dear? Are you and Erick having a tiff?" She circles me with concern.

"Fighting? What? No. Not at all. I hadn't thought about it. I loved that ring because of the special history with you and Odell." I bounce my shoulders once. "I'm not sure I want jewelry just for the sake of jewelry."

"Mizithra! It's not jewelry! A wedding ring is a symbol of the never-ending bond of love between you and Erick. It's important. You can at least make the effort to have an opinion." Her glowing eyes flicker as she hovers in front of me.

"All right. Easy, Cujo." Calling to mind images from the stack of bridal magazines my step-mother, Amaryllis, kept sharing with me, I ponder my options. "If I had to choose, I think I'd go with rose gold and a fire-opal center stone.

Maybe a few diamonds, but not as the main thing."

Ghost-ma nods her approval. "I like your style, sweetie. Now you'll be—"

BING. BONG. BING.

"You expecting a delivery, dear?"

"Me? I'm pretty much never expecting a delivery." However, I get to my feet and take a step toward the twisted ivy medallion of plaster that serves as the button for the hidden door.

Despite my grandmother's insinuation about my psychic abilities, I had no premonition about the doorbell beside the alleyway door or who might be ringing it.

"Sometimes you get premonitions or messages."

Kicking out one hip, I plant a fist on it and, with the other hand, point sternly to my closed lips. "No. Thought. Dropping."

"Oh, Mitzy."

No point in beating that dead horse. Grams has already pummeled its ghost with her excuses.

There's an indignant scoff in my wake as I trudge down the circular staircase and head to the side door.

Bracing myself against the blast of cold air that will certainly be whistling down my alley and carrying a flurry of snow with it, I push open the door. "Tadjo Nowak?"

"Mitzy, I'm so glad you're here. I'm distraught. I'm utterly distraught!" His slouchy robin's egg-blue beanie pairs nicely with his teal scarf and gloves.

For the life of me, I can't imagine why the son of our local gypsy witch — my grandmother's lifelong rival — is knocking at my door at this hour. Luckily, I've learned a few manners since I landed in almost-Canada. "Come in. Come in."

He steps into the building, and I usher him to the back room as the eternal barista in me pushes brew on the ancient coffeemaker in the corner. "What happened? Why are you so upset?"

"I had to go to New York for a few days. A possible show — Tony potential. Meetings. Investors. You know the drill!"

I'm not that familiar with Broadway, but as a film-school dropout, I'm quite familiar with the development drill. Lots of people making promises they never plan on keeping. Money is always talked about in vague terms, and everyone's expensing lunches. I'll spare you my dreary summary. "Sure. So what happened?"

"In New York? The usual. I've got a couple deals simmering away, and my agent tells me I'm in desperate need of a new hit."

"Understood. Why are you distraught?" Apparently I'm going to need to be more specific if I plan to keep this drama queen on point.

"Yes. Thank you for keeping me on task." Tadjo tugs at the beanie and accepts a cup of coffee. "You would be an excellent producer's assistant. Have you ever thought about a career on The Great White Way?"

"Thanks, really, but I'm happy here. The bookshop, the PI business, I'm busy — the right amount busy."

"Yes, Ray told me about your PI business." He takes a sip and forces a smile. The quality of my brew is clearly beneath him, despite his efforts to appear grateful. "But my mother is the reason I'm here."

His brother Ray works at the local hospital, and together, the two of them are caring for their elderly mother, who used to be my grandmother's archrival. No one holds a grudge like a Polish gypsy. "How is your mother?"

"Dead! She's dead, Mitzy."

Didn't see that coming. That's two surprises for the psychic in one day. Maybe I'm slipping.

"What? I thought the treatments were helping her. I mean, mostly with quality of life, but I hoped maybe she was getting better, right?"

"Oh! When I think about everything I gave up to be here. To help her." He clutches his expertly looped scarf.

"Tadjo, how did your mother die?"

"Did I say dead? I don't mean to exaggerate. It was early this morning. I hadn't even had my third cup of coffee . . . Although, she *was* barely breathing. When the paramedics rolled her out of the shop, I might've heard the heart machine stop beeping." He throws his arms in the air and takes an emotional lap around my tiny bistro table as I refill my coffee.

Classic theater folk. "So probably not dead. What happened?"

"Absolutely. No. Idea." He presses a hand to his chest and exhales with force. "When I left the hospital, she was still unconscious."

"Why don't you start at the beginning?"

He immediately places his mug on the table and continues his well-rehearsed gesticulating.

"The shop was dark. I put my key in the lock, but the door was already open." He pauses, arches a brow, and continues, "When I stepped through—" He claws at his chest and vamps for the invisible audience. "I sensed it before I turned on the light. There she was—" He chokes on a sob and grasps one of my old wooden chairs with both hands as he leans heavily and attempts to squeeze out a teardrop.

None fall.

"What did you find?" It's all I can do to resist using one of the alchemical workings Silas taught me for snatching answers from the subject's subconscious. I'm sure I could do it. Maybe a couple of deep breaths . . .

"My mother was lying on the floor motionless. Before I even touched her, I knew it was bad. I called 911. Sheriff Paulsen and one of the deputies arrived before the paramedics. She'd heard my mother had 'rages' before and claimed the state of the shop was due to one of my mother's moods. Too much for an old woman's heart, Paulsen said. Looked like natural causes—" Once again, he chokes back a silent sob and works on those nonexistent tears.

"I feel like there's more to this story, Tadjo. That's why you're here, right?"

"My mother always said you were different. Like her, but different. When the paramedics arrived, they located a faint pulse. They claimed it was a heart attack and rushed her to the hospital. But the state of the shop! I don't think what happened to my matka had anything to do with natural causes. I think the causes were supernatural, if you get my drift?"

Don't ask me how, but some part of my psychic brain knows that "matka" means mother, and Tadjo's mother is a powerful witch. The hairs on the back of my neck stand on end, and finally, my extrasensory perceptions fully kick in.

"Describe the scene."

He tilts his head and looks at me as though I invited him to tea with the queen. "This is exactly why I'm hiring you!"

I was getting that vibe, but it's nice to hear him say it out loud. "Go on."

"You know my mother's shop. Incense, crystals, occult items . . . Things were strewn all about. Books pulled from bookshelves, statues cracked . . . The place looked like a cyclone had passed through."

Before the current detente had been reached between Ania Karina Nowak and my grandmother, I had witnessed such a battle between the powerful gypsy and my alchemical mentor, Silas Willoughby. However, I knew Silas would not go looking for a fight. He uses his powers only in the defense of the innocent — or protection of me.

"Was anything missing?"

"I don't know. Maybe you can help me with inventory?"

"Was there anything in your mother's hand?"

Tadjo stops and gazes up to the left. Accessing an actual memory. "She had her cane in her left hand, but she always carried that."

"How was she holding it?" There's a swirling in my stomach that I don't want to acknowledge.

"What a strange question. She was holding it in the middle. Not at the top. She was—"

"She was wielding it as a weapon against an enemy."

"But she wouldn't. She has no enemies."

Externally, I shrug my shoulders, but in my gut I know the truth. Ania Karina Nowak may not admit to having enemies, but I know of at least one unhappy customer.

Brandi Schloss.

Although Brandi is currently doing twenty-five-to-life in a ward for the criminally insane for her deadly antics at the Fox Mountain Ski Resort, my point stands. Ania Karina had enemies, whether Tadjo wants to admit it or not.

CHAPTER 2

AFTER PROMISING Tadjo I'd stop by the Emporium and assist him with inventory, I race up to the Rare Books Loft and shout for Grams and Pyewacket.

Shockingly, they both appear without complaint.

Pyewacket leaps onto the sturdy oak reading table beside me in a blur of tan glory, and his black-tufted ears twitch in anticipation.

"I've got to call Silas. But you all need to hear this."

Now that the gang is assembled, I press speed dial for *Secret Alchemist* and wait.

"Good morning, Mizithra. You've risen quite early. To what do I owe the pleasure?"

"It's not good news. I mean, good morning, Mr. Willoughby."

"There's distress in your voice. Are you unharmed?"

"For now."

Grams gasps, and her glowing apparition floats closer.

"Tadjo Nowak was just here. There was an attempt on his mother's life. Of course, Paulsen thinks the incident is a result of natural causes, but the scene he described says otherwise. Someone, or *someones*, trashed her shop and left her for dead."

Silas harrumphs, and I can easily see him smoothing his bushy grey mustache with a thumb and forefinger. "Shall I join you?"

"Nah. I'm headed over to Ania's Emporium. I promised Tadjo I'd help him with inventory. I figured you'd want to know if there's anything missing. Tossing the place could've been a cover, right?"

"Indeed. Be on your guard, Mizithra. This is perhaps only the first step in a complicated plan of deception. Are you wearing your mother's dream-catcher necklace?"

"Yeah."

"And the key? The key to the main entrance of Bell, Book & Candle Bookshop?"

"No, but I'll grab it before I go to the Emporium. Is it important?"

"Of the utmost." Silas ends the call, and I hurry back to the walk-up.

Grams insists I hold the door for her and invite her in — the only way she can gain access to the private residence Erick and I share. When we remodeled the old printing museum into a three-story home to begin our new life, I asked Silas to place wards and sigils that would keep Ghost-ma from popping in at will. Nothing against my wonderful apparition of a grandmother, but newlyweds do need privacy.

In the third-floor primary suite, I hurry to the bedside table, open a drawer and reach in. The large brass key, with its unique triangular barrel, has intricate markings on all sides. The weight of it in my hand always calms me. I slip the chain around my neck and tuck the key under my layers, to rest heavy beside the necklace from my mother.

"I better get over to that new-age shop and see if Tadjo and I can figure out what's missing. I know for a fact the attack on his mother was no accident. And there's absolutely no way Ania Karina nearly died protecting a mundane crystal or packet of incense."

"You're absolutely right, sweetie. We both know that woman carries some questionable and unusual items. Think about what happened to your stepbrother's girlfriend."

"Technically, it happened to her dog. But we figured it all out." The camera that turned a basenji into a ghost is another story.

"I'll let you know if we find anything. Can you leave a note for—? Never mind. I'm gonna call Twiggy and tell her not to open the bookshop today."

Turning to Pyewacket, I gaze deeply into his wise, golden eyes. "Be on the lookout for any sign of trouble, son. Keep Grams safe, all right?"

"RE-OW!" Game on!

Grabbing my outerwear, I hurry down the alley, type in the code to open my garage door, and un-plug the cord from my Jeep. Plugging in non-elec-tric cars in the winter is a unique experience. Erick explained something about keeping the oil warm — but I didn't pay much attention.

Grabbing the keys from under the visor, I bring the engine to life and head out. The four-wheel-drive is exactly what I'll need to get me safely to the trinket shop.

Pulling into the parking lot at Ania's Empo-rium, the sight of crime-scene tape brings a swirl of sadness.

We had our run-ins, but once we smoothed things over, I hoped I might learn something from her. A part of me even imagined taking it a step be-yond reconciliation and creating a friendship. Time flies. You never know how long you have with someone.

If she pulls through . . .

When I reach for the handle of the front door, I have to step back to avoid being knocked over.

Short, squat Sheriff Paulsen bursts out to confront me in a swirl of brown polyester. Her right hand firmly grips the handle of the gun in her holster. "No. No. No. You load into your vehicle and drive straight back to your private investigator agency. I don't need you contaminating my crime scene."

"I wouldn't dream of contaminating your crime scene. Actually, I heard you suspected no foul play, so I can't quite figure out why you're calling it a crime scene."

That one stumps her for a moment.

"New information has come to light. I don't need to discuss an ongoing investigation with you."

"That's correct. Although, I'll be happy to discuss one with you when I uncover additional clues."

The sheriff's grip tightens on the handle of her gun, and I worry I may have pushed too hard.

Luckily, Tadjo waltzes out of the shop and flings one end of his scarf over his shoulder. "Mitzy! Thank goodness you're here. Come in. Come in."

Scrunching up my face, I shrug and slip past

the angry sheriff. "Don't worry, Paulsen, I'm only here to help with inventory."

"I better not hear different." She sucks air in between her clenched teeth.

My grandmother's voice echoes in my head, "You get more flies with honey, dear." And though I'd like to tell Paulsen, she rarely hears anything that doesn't smack her upside the head. I choose to hold my witty tongue. However, as I enter the shop, I mentally pat myself on the back for being such a grown-up today.

The tinkling chimes that usually sound when you open the door have been removed, but the heady aromas of incense, soaps, herbs, and oils hit me like a brick wall.

Tadjo snags my hand and pulls me through the beaded curtain into the back room. "This is going to be tough. My mother was absolutely anti-technology." He rolls his eyes and shakes his head from side to side.

"We'll be fine. This whole town seems to have missed the technology revolution. What are we working with?"

He pulls four three-inch-thick three-ring binders from a shelf and stacks them on the table between us one by one. "This is her system. She keeps handwritten invoices of everything she orders. Then she comes in and writes the date of sale beside each item as it leaves the store."

I sense he's not finished. "And?"

"And they're organized by date. Not by type of merchandise. Not by any category. By date." His shoulders slump, and he exhales loudly as he tugs on his slouched beanie.

"All righty. This will sure be fun." I can't mention to Tadjo that my extrasensory abilities might help us narrow things down. Once Paulsen clears out of the retail area, I'll walk through and use some techniques Silas has taught me to investigate the residual energy. He refers to it as forensic alchemy. I simply call it a cool trick. Well, not in front of him.

Tadjo slides one of the thick binders across the table. "You start with this one, and I'll start with this one. Seems like we'll be here all day. Let me know if you need me to order lunch."

Blerg. "Hey, I forgot to call Erick. I was supposed to— Give me a minute."

Stepping out the back door, I call my husband and bring him up to speed on the unfortunate events of the morning.

"I can be there in five."

"It's not necessary. Honestly. Tadjo and I can get through the inventory."

"I'm sure you can. And I absolutely trust every one

of your special abilities, Moon. Thing is, I have years of experience investigating crime scenes. Plus, I can keep Tadjo out of your hair if you need to use your powers."

"Looks like you're jockeying for the husband of the year award again, Harper."

He chuckles. "Possibly. How's it looking?"

As images of Detective Too-Hot-To-Handle dance through my head, I shiver — and not from the cold. "Fine. Get over here and run interference for me. The sooner we figure out what's missing, the sooner I can get Silas researching the right thing. His hypothesis is that this could be the first step in a complicated supernatural plan, and we're not gonna know how to battle it until we figure out what that is. Definitely all hands on deck. Thanks."

"See you soon, wife-y."

What a smart aleck. He's lucky he has other irresistible qualities. Like—

Focus up! This is an investigation, not a slumber party.

Shoot! Now I'm picturing Erick shirtless in a pair of those sexy drawstring flannel pajama pants.

The back door swings open. "Mitzy? You okay? You're flushed." Tadjo tilts his head in concern.

Gulp.

"I'm fine. Let's hit those books."

Yeesh.

CHAPTER 3

By the time Erick arrives at Ania's Emporium, Tadjo has made it through two pages and I've made it through three. A staggeringly pathetic accomplishment in the face of all that remains.

"Hey, you must be Tadjo." My husband extends his hand. "Erick Harper. Nice to meet you."

"Weren't you the sheriff?" Tadjo smiles warmly and looks Erick up and down.

"I was. But once Mitzy and I got married, we decided a joint venture would be better for both of us."

The young Mr. Nowak flashes his eyebrows at me. "That was some wedding, darling! I'm telling you right now, I used several of the pictures I took at your ceremony and reception to enhance my vision board."

"I have my Grams to—" My eyes go wide, and my gaze darts to Erick.

"She takes after her grandmother. Great taste and an eye for fashion."

Tadjo lifts one shoulder and nods slowly as a knowing grin spreads across his face. "Right. I'm sure that's what she meant."

An uneasy silence hangs between us. This guy is not as easy to fool as most people. He's had his share of exposure to the paranormal during his up-bringing. Ania Karina is a supernatural force to be reckoned with . . .

"Would you mind walking me through the scene out here?" Erick is asking Tadjo the question, but his eyes connect with me. This is my chance to let my abilities loose on the beastly volumes of inventory.

The young man adjusts his scarf and touches Erick's arm. "I'd be happy to. Follow me."

Oh brother. I'm lucky my husband is a modest man. Otherwise, all of this over-the-top attention from uptown Mr. Nowak might go to his head.

As soon as the guys pass beyond the beaded curtain, it's time to let my freak flag fly. I lay all four books on the table. Silently pleading with the moody mood ring on my left hand, I beg for assistance in eliminating some of the drudgery.

Lifting my left hand above the books and taking several deep breaths, I quiet my mind and focus.

The smoky black cabochon encircled by gold braid turns icy cold. I move my hand over the next book and experience no change. As my hand approaches the third book, the ring heats, and when I slide across to the fourth book, the temperature cools.

Sweet. Now we're down to one book. Now what? I don't have time to wave the ring over each page.

Opening the book to the middle, I hold my hand over the left side — heat. Move it to the right — cool.

All right. I have a strategy. Marking my place with the right hand. I divide another section and flip them over. This time, left — cool. Right — warm.

Continuing in this way, I eventually get to a handwritten invoice containing a list of seven items. This will definitely be easier than four books of inventory.

Of the seven items listed, two are marked as sold. One last year and one the year before that. Fine. That leaves five items to be identified and searched for in the shop.

Snapping open the shiny silver D-rings, I remove the page and stroll out of the back room.

"Hey Tadjo, can you help me find a few things?"

He smiles. "So you think you've got a winner there, darling?"

Shrugging, I fan the page. "I have a good feeling about this."

He angles his head back and squints one eye. "I know what that means. Let me check." Tadjo takes the sheet from my hand and runs a finger down. "The amulet of Horus." He moves to the counter supporting the cash register, and points. "Right there. Some people think it's an ankh, but they're not the same thing. Let's see . . ." He runs his finger down the list. "Lapis lazuli replica sarcophagus." He strolls over to a section of the wall that took serious damage. Crouching, he sorts through several items on the floor. "Found it."

Glancing at Erick, I give him a surreptitious thumbs up. He shrugs. Yup. He's definitely out of his comfort zone.

"The 9 x 12 painting of Petra." Tadjo turns in a half-circle and points to the wall behind the jewelry counter. "Still there."

He continues down the list. "Eye of the Priestess." Leaning his left ear toward his shoulder, he repeats the movement to the right. "I remember my mother was very excited about that one. She placed it in some kind of container. It was a stone box or wooden chest."

Erick and I fan out, looking for anything that fits the description.

After opening several wooden chests to discover various crystals or statuettes of Quan Yin, I turn to the guys. "Anything?"

My husband straightens and shrugs his shoulders. "I've checked all the boxes over here. Nothing looks like an eye."

Tadjo sighs dejectedly. "No luck here either."

"Was that the last item?" Erick glances toward me, but Tadjo replies.

"Nope. The last item is the orb of Osiris."

For some reason, a golden sphere tucked under some rubble catches my eye. Stepping toward it, I slowly lift it into the air. "Could this be it?"

Tadjo smiles. "A-maaah-zing! You're fantastic at this, Mitzy. You and I definitely should work together."

"Thanks, but I have a job — and a partner."

Erick chuckles as we each walk one last lap around the perimeter of the store. Every psychic ability I have is tingling with knowledge. "Tadjo, I'm pretty sure the missing item is the Eye of the Priestess. What do you know about it?"

He taps two fingers on his chin and mumbles something under his breath.

"What was that?" I couldn't quite make out his grumbling.

"Nothing I can remember. My matka always said I was a poor pupil. She accused me of having my head in the stars." He sighs and presses a hand to his chest. "Can you imagine?"

To Erick's credit, he maintains a stoic expression. I, on the other hand, am forced to hide my snicker in a feigned fit of coughing.

"I can't." A giggle disguised as a throat clearing follows. "Mothers, right?" I shrug.

Hubby to the rescue. "I'll walk you out, Moon."

Slipping my arm through the crook of Erick's elbow, I toss a final comment over my shoulder as we head out. "Let me know if that 'eye' thing-y turns up, or if you remember anything about it."

Tadjo tugs on the fringe of his scarf and his thoughts seem far away.

"You'll call, right?"

He snaps to and nods. "Why, of course."

The inflection is convincing, but the blank stare leaves me wondering.

Theater people.

CHAPTER 4

ERICK WALKS me to the Jeep and leans down to plant a kiss on my cheek. "I'm gonna park the Nova at home and walk to the office. See you there."

Sounds like I'll be going to the office. Hooray.

As I pull out of the parking lot and head toward our First Avenue PI office, memories of past cases flood through my mind.

After reviewing the extrasensory data, I come to the conclusion that I'm much stronger and better trained than when I had to face Rory Bombay. I know I can help Silas against this new threat — if he'll let me. There has to be a way to gain his confidence.

The small parking lot outside Harper and Moon Investigations is as empty as my list of plans to convince Silas to accept my help.

Oh great. I don't have my key to the office. Wow, I'm already inspiring confidence.

Blerg.

I'll have to leave the car running to keep the heater toasting my feet. Feels like I could turn into a human icicle in minutes out there.

Erick jogs into the parking lot, points to me in the car, and shrugs.

This guy! Jogging in the winter! I mean, technically it's spring, but let's be honest, this is winter weather. As I exit my vehicle, he chuckles. "I thought you'd be inside brewing up the coffee."

"Hilarious. I forgot my key. Plus, I haven't eaten, and I thought maybe—"

"Back in the vehicle, Moon. Let's get you over to Myrtle's Diner before you fade away. You can't be expected to work on an empty stomach."

Grinning like a spoiled child, I climb back in the Jeep.

When we step into the comforting aromas and the warmth of the diner named after my grandmother, my granddad offers a spatula salute through the red-Formica-trimmed orders-up window.

"Hey, Gramps!"

The creases deepen around his eyes as he chuckles.

Erick and I slide into our favorite corner booth,

and I toss one more zinger at my hubby. "Thanks for joining me on my state-mandated lunch break."

"I have to keep my employees happy, don't I?"

"Rude."

He walks his fingers across the table and turns his palm up. Placing my hand in his, I smile as he rubs the back of my hand. "I was only teasing, Moon. We're fifty-fifty partners in the business — and in life. I'd be useless without you."

"That's the most brilliant thing you've said all day." I love the way his blue eyes sparkle when he's bantering with me. Dead sexy.

Detective Too-Hot-To-Handle laughs easily and leans back against the red-vinyl bench seat. His gaze darts toward the door, and a strange, mischievous grin tugs at the corner of his pouty mouth.

"Do I even want to turn around?"

He inhales deeply. "She's headed this way."

Curiosity gets the best of me, which is, I'm sure, what will be chiseled on my headstone, and I turn to look toward the door. Moving hesitantly in our direction is a young woman in an instantly recognizable jester-style beanie.

Quickly turning away, I mouth at Erick, "Is that Bristol?"

He waves. "Hey, Bristol."

She rushes to our table and pulls off her stocking cap. A few wild coffee-brown hairs escape from her braids and dance with static electricity as she bows. "Mitzy. It's an honor."

It makes me kind of uncomfortable when she acts like she's meeting royalty. At least she didn't kneel this time. I wave off the action with both hands. "Come on, Bristol. We're way past that. I may not exactly be thrilled with the blog you're running about the cases I solve, but you were a big help on the snowmobile murder."

She shakes her head. "No way. I did nothing, man. It was totally you. Totally you, being completely next level, as always."

Having a fangirl at point-blank range makes me terribly self-conscious. "Well, thanks. Are you here to eat, or was there something else?"

"Um— So— It's—"

"Bristol, spit it out. Whatever it is, it looks like it's killing you." I smile encouragingly.

"Excuse me, kid."

Bristol steps aside so Odell can place our plates on the table. With May just around the corner, we're about to enter taco-salad season for my husband, but it's still April, and with the cold temperatures, I'm pretty sure my grandfather made the right call in delivering meatloaf and mashed potatoes. I eagerly slide my cheeseburger and fries in front of me and dig right in.

Odell raps his knuckles twice on the tabletop and returns to the kitchen.

Bristol steps back to the booth. "So, like, you guys opened a detective agency."

Swallowing a mouthful of delicious golden french fries, I offer a correction. "Private investigations. What's your point?"

"So, like, I know you guys work the cases together. Maybe you need someone in the office. Like to help, or whatever." She fumbles her jester's cap from one hand to the other.

"Bristol, honey, is there a question in there somewhere?"

"Are you hiring?"

My eyes widen in a "please let this not be true" expression as I stare across the table at my partner.

Erick, ever the levelheaded, asks the follow-up question. "Do you have any admin experience?"

She launches into an explanation of all the duties involved in running her blog, including the number of followers — which is much larger than I would've hoped — the sponsored deals she secures from advertisers, and on and on.

Erick smiles. "That's truly impressive, Bristol. Why don't you drop off a resumé later today? Mitzy and I will mull it over. I don't think we're quite busy enough to need the help, but we won't be able to take on more cases until we have help. Bit of a Catch-22."

The blank expression on her youthful face is a clear indication that she's not old enough to have seen the movie or read the book.

"No doubt. Thanks. You guys are the best. Like, seriously smashing it." She whips out her phone, taps the camera into selfie-mode, and turns her back to us as she announces, "POV: applying for a job at the best detective agency in town!"

Oh brother.

Oddly, Bristol fails to exit after her amazing selfie. She shoves her phone in her pocket and shifts her weight from one snow boot to the other.

"Okay, cool. You guys are working on that Emporium case, right?"

I exchange a look with Erick that says don't mention anything . . . At least, that's what it says from my side of the table. Apparently, reception across the silver-flecked white Formica is a little sketchy.

He sniffs sharply and leans toward Bristol. "We haven't made anything official. What did you hear?"

Bristol shrugs and looks at her feet. "So, like, I blogged about the police beat before — you know."

Erick shakes his head. "Before what?"

She peers at me from the corner of her eye, and

I can sense she's about to drop on her knee and sing my praises.

"Bristol, please don't make a scene. If you're referring to 'before I came to town,' we're all up to speed. What does that have to do with you knowing about the Emporium? The official story was a heart attack." No need to tell her about Tadjo acquiring our services this morning.

She bobs her head. "Right. But that's pretty sus. Like, one minute the witch is Gucci, the next minute she's sorta corpse."

"She's recovering in the hospital, Bristol. What's your point?"

"Um, so, I have a police scanner. It was how I got the information for my blog." She wrings her beanie in her hands.

Glancing at Erick, I arch an eyebrow, and he nods.

"So what did you hear on the police scanner, Bristol?" He leans back and waits patiently.

She rolls her head back and forth, continuing the assault on the headwear in her grip. "So, like, Paulsen was telling one of the deputies to keep Moon away from the crime scene."

My mouth drops like the drawbridge on a medieval castle, while my husband chuckles at my expense. Erick takes a long, thoughtful sip of coffee and smiles at Bristol. "So you deduced that if

Paulsen was attempting to keep Moon from the scene, Harper and Moon were on the case?"

Her gaze pops from the floor, and she fixes Erick with wide brown eyes. "Can I use that on the blog? That's a bussin' tagline."

Erick smiles and tilts his head. "Sure. You write what you want, Bristol. I believe in freedom of the press."

"Noice."

Seems like she's got us dead to rights. "Since we're officially talking about this case, did you have some information to share, Bristol?" She glances toward me, and once again, I sense her need to pledge her fealty. I hustle to intercept. "Just stay on your feet. Whatever you need to tell me is between friends, all right?"

Her big brown eyes brim with admiration.

I'm having serious trouble dealing with one super fan. I can't imagine what I'd do if all the people who actually read her blog descended on Pin Cherry Harbor.

"No doubt. Here's the fresh juice. Mr. Nowak, the big Broadway director, came to talk to Mr. Ball's theater tech class at BC3."

Watching the confusion swirl across Erick's face as he attempts to decipher Bristol's shorthand amuses me. Birch County Community College always seems like a mouthful, and its acronym,

BCCC, isn't much better. I appreciate her ability to create a succinct abbreviation that's also kinda fun to say.

She waits for me to nod before continuing. "He was telling us about the big shows he's put on, how many Tonys he won, and some new show he's got on simmer. Then he, like, asked for any questions, and this full-on tool in the audience said, 'Hey, isn't your mom a witch?'"

Glancing at Erick, I attempt to shake my head as subtly as possible before I reply. The last thing we need is a wild story about witches circulating through the gossip mill and interfering with our investigation. "What did Tadjo, I mean, Mr. Nowak, say?"

"He was super chill. Said that his matka — prolly some Polish word for mother — came from a proud line of traveling people who had studied homeopathic healing. It was a pretty clutch answer."

"What did the smart-aleck kid say?"

"Dude was cold. He said that place shouldn't be selling shady potions. And that he heard about some kid who got super tilted off one of her brews and tried to kill himself or something. Then he spilled more low-key insults about her being a witch or whatever. Mr. Nowak just ignored him and took other questions. But Nowak looked kinda pissed."

Arching an eyebrow, I attempt to gentrify our young friend. "I'm sure you meant to say upset, right?"

She nearly rips her jester's beanie in half as she struggles to contain the bubbling embarrassment. "Oh for sure, for sure. Salty. I shoulda said salty."

Across the table, Erick can barely hide his amusement. "Thanks for the information, Bristol. We'll definitely follow up on that lead."

She bows twice as she backs away. "Can I quote you on that?"

He sighs heavily. "Of course." Erick waves and nods. "We'll see you later, Bristol."

I'm too speechless to act.

"You totally will." She pulls her hat on and bounces out — pom-poms be-bopping on her cap as she exits.

CHAPTER 5

My conscience gets the better of me, and I have to forgo logging more hours at Harper and Moon Investigations in favor of a return to the bookshop.

Dropping Erick at the office, I drive the short distance to Bell, Book & Candle to update Grams and Pyewacket.

Entering through the side door, I trudge up to my old apartment, calling out for my cohorts as I go.

By the time I tilt the candle handle next to my copy of *Saducismus Triumphatus*, Pyewacket is winding figure eights through my legs as Grams pokes her head through the wall.

"Get the murder board ready, Grams."

"Who's dead?"

"At this point, it was only attempted murder.

What we have to figure out now is why. That will hopefully take us to 'who.'"

"Fine. Who's almost-murder are we solving?"

"Only our favorite new-age shop owner, Ania Karina Nowak."

There's a spiteful twinkle in Ghost-ma's eye, but she recovers nicely. "I'm sorry to hear that. How are her sons taking it?"

"I haven't spoken to Ray, but Tadjo is definitely taking to the role of tragically inconvenienced son with the gusto of a true former Broadway star."

Grams giggles. "You better go feed Mr. Cuddlekins. He's clearly half-starved. He hasn't made a peep since you arrived."

"Copy that. Follow me, Pye. We'll get you a nice heaping bowl of Fruity Puffs. Sound good?"

My wily caracal drops an item at my feet before responding. "Reow." Can confirm.

Stooping, I pick up a toy baby bottle. "Robin Pyewacket Goodfellow, you better not be working with Ghost-ma to pressure me into childrearing."

His black-tufted ears twitch, and he squeezes his eyes closed.

"Fine. Suit yourself, demon spawn." I toss the bottle in a trash bin at the bottom of the stairs and receive a loud reproach.

"Ree-OW!" A warning punctuated by a threat.

Have you ever been face-to-whiskers with a

genuine wildcat? When he's furious? Not great for the nerves.

Removing the bottle from the trashcan, I tuck it in my back pocket. "I'll hang onto this important clue, M'lord."

When we reach the back room, I'm horrified to discover only a single box of his favorite sugary children's cereal in the cupboard. It's nearly empty, and there are no backups. I choose to keep this information to myself, but Pyewacket narrows his gaze, and his golden eyes seem to see straight through me.

Bending, I empty the box into his bowl. "Don't worry, I'll stop by the Piggly Wiggly and pick up a fresh supply when I grab Erick from the office. You won't starve on my watch, your royal furriness."

At official headquarters, Grams has successfully moved the rolling corkboard to the center of the room and is in the process of filling out 3 x 5 cards for Ania, her husband, and the sons.

"You don't suspect a family member, do you?"

"You know our motto, dear. Everyone's a suspect until they're not. I realize it might seem more obvious to suspect some mysterious rival witch, but you know what they say. If you only have a hammer, you're always looking for nails."

"Look, I can guarantee that Tadjo didn't attempt to kill his mother. But if it makes you feel better, you can write all the cards you want."

"Well, aren't we looking for connections, sweetie? Maybe there's someone in the Nowak's present who might have a grudge against the family. Who knows what lengths someone might go to — to get to them."

The mood ring on my left hand burns a fiery circle around my ring finger. "Grams, do you remember that guy who posed as a magician in Broken Rock and turned out to be Erick's bio dad? Alex Crenshaw? There's an image of him in the mood ring. What could that mean?"

She floats around the corkboard in a slow circle as she twists at a ruby ring on her right hand in silent thought.

Finally, she offers an idea. "Erick spoke to him a few months ago, right? Do you think there could be more information about the strange assistant, Artemis Ward? Maybe Erick should check again?"

"Right. Hopefully, I can talk him into taking me along for another interview. I'm bound to pick up on something that Erick might miss."

"I believe that, Mitzy. But maybe it doesn't have anything to do with talking to him at all. Alex Crenshaw is the link between you and that power-hungry Artemis Ward."

"What do you mean? Why would that link to me? Why not to Erick?"

"Think about it, darling. As wonderful as Erick

is — and you know I think he's the tops — he's not special, like you. Alex links to Erick, and that links directly to you. If Artemis Ward is searching for ways to steal mystical knowledge and increase her powers, maybe she's not looking for Silas."

"Grams, get a hold of yourself. She took out two members of a secret society. If Jedediah hadn't already passed of natural causes, Mr. Willoughby's brother would've been her third victim. If she's responsible for this attack on Ania Karina, then she's only back in town for one reason: Silas."

"Possibly. Then again, I've learned it's dangerous to count your chickens before they're hatched." She taps one perfectly manicured finger on her coral lip.

"Fair enough. Make a card for Alex Crenshaw. I don't know how it connects to anything, but we both know this ring is far too moody to show me things for no reason."

Grams scribbles out another card and passes it to me.

Before I can make heads or tails of the dodgy evidence before us, the hidden bookcase door slides open behind us, and I let out a scream.

"Easy, Moon. It's only me."

Turning to look over the back of the settee, I breathe an enormous sigh of relief when I see Erick Harper in all his six-foot-and-change glory.

"I was going to come back to the office to pick you up."

"No big deal. It's actually pretty nice out. I enjoyed the walk."

"You're nuts, Harper. It's freezing outside, and you'll never convince me otherwise."

Erick glances toward the murder board. "Did the woman from the Emporium pass away?"

"No. But she's clearly not out of the woods. We're taking it as an attempted murder and the possible theft of a powerful paranormal item. We need to get ahead of this thing."

He nods. "Fine by me. How can I help?"

Pyewacket leaps onto the settee and places an insistent paw on my leg. "My furry overlord requires sustenance. We emptied the last box of Fruity Puffs earlier. He's been inconsolable ever since."

Erick chuckles. "Don't worry, buddy. I have an emergency box in the walk-up. I'll get that 'just in case' box before I head over to the grocery store to grab something for dinner."

"I'm not sure if you're trying to get brownie points with me or Pye?" Crossing my arms, I wait for my husband's reassurance. Instead, he pulls a "Mitzy" and comes straight out of left field.

"Should we talk to Tadjo about the obnoxious

student Bristol mentioned, or just head over to BCCC tomorrow?"

It's impossible to prevent my eyes from rolling back in my head. "As I've mentioned before, we can simply call it the community college. There's just the one. We'll both know what you're talking about. And I say we head straight over there. Tadjo isn't going to have any idea who the kid was, but I feel certain the theater tech professor is quite familiar with all of his rowdy ne'er-do-wells."

Erick smirks as he walks toward the exit. "You look like a gal who's quite familiar with the moniker *ne'er-do-well*. Am I right?"

"Touché."

He presses the twisted ivy medallion, and as the hidden door slides open behind him, he calls out, "What are you making for dinner, Moon?"

Plot twist. "Let's see. I've learned to make a mean tuna noodle hot dish, slightly burned pancakes, and I thought I did a decent job on the roasted chicken."

He laughs warmly and drags his thumb along his stubbled jaw. "If memory serves, you bought a pre-roasted chicken from the Piggly Wiggly. That doesn't really count as cooking."

"Hey, properly using the resources at my disposal is a form of cooking."

Erick arches one eyebrow. "If you say so, my darling heiress. After I stock up on Fruity Puffs at the Piggly Wiggly, should I grab takeout at the Red Door?"

Chinese food is one of my all-time favorites. "Fair play to you, Harper. You know what I like."

His eyes dart around the room. "Are we alone?"

Gesturing toward the rolling corkboard, I shake my head. "Not even close. Grams is swirling around the attempted-murder wall, and Pyewacket is practically a pro at eavesdropping."

"Then I'll revisit this conversation about what you like at a later date."

A flush of tingles from head to toe causes me to shiver. "Uh oh."

His chuckles drift across the Rare Books Loft and disappear as the door slides shut behind him.

Whew. That man has a dangerous way with words!

Grams drifts toward me. "If your not-so-secret thoughts are any indication, that man has a way with far more than words." Her ethereal eyes sparkle.

"Get out of my head, woman!"

She chuckles as she rearranges the cards on the corkboard.

For the moment, it seems like Harper and Moon are ahead of the case. Wonder how long that will last?

CHAPTER 6

THE THEATER BUILDING is simple to locate. The sloping, windowless roof, towering above the stage, is a dead giveaway.

Heading around to the side of the enormous structure, we enter through doors that lead to classrooms and offices rather than the spacious performance hall.

Our local community college fine arts department isn't an enormous venture. It's not difficult to locate the office of Mr. Ball.

Erick knocks. Not a cop knock. A gentle, friendly, inquiring knock.

The door opens, and a puff of stale, coffee-scented air wafts into the hall.

"May I help you?" This guy is a textbook theater professor. Slightly unkempt hair, glasses teetering on the tip of his nose, and his tweed coat has the obligatory leather patches at each elbow. I'm seriously going to enjoy chatting with Mr. Ball.

Gesturing to his small office, I paste on my best smile. "Can we chat in private? We only need a moment of your valuable time."

My thinly veiled attempt to flatter my way in succeeds. Mr. Ball points to two well-worn blue chairs and takes a seat in his enormous leather rolly chair.

Attempting to hold my false grin in place, I continue. "Hi, Mr. Ball. Thank you for seeing us. We're investigating the attempted murder of a local resident. Following up every lead. I hope you understand."

Mr. Ball tugs on the cuffs of his shirt and crosses his arms. The fingers of his left hand brush the leather elbow patch of his jacket. "I can assure you I'd have nothing to do with something as mundane as murder."

Wow. It's true what they say about theater folk. They definitely have a looser grip on reality than the rest of us. I can't think of a single time in my life when I would've considered murder mundane.

Thankfully, Erick accepts the interview baton in my silence.

"Mr. Ball, you are in no way a suspect. We'd like to ask about one of your students."

The professor's arms uncross, and he inhales sharply. "Now there's the next hit Broadway show! Which one of those miscreants do you suspect?"

My long-suffering husband smiles pleasantly. "Just following leads at this point, Mr. Ball. Anything you can tell us would be greatly appreciated." He waits for the professor to consent.

He receives no such word or gesture. Instead, a sharp sniff and a re-crossing of the arms.

Erick proceeds. "Mr. Nowak was speaking to your class the other day when one of your students began heckling him. Can you tell us the name of that student?"

"That would be Tayton Vrieswyk. The dimmest bulb in the show."

Something in the back of my little psychic brain tingles at the name. "Tayton? Isn't he a hotshot hockey player?"

You would think I offered the professor a plate of raw frog legs. He grimaces and shivers as he looks away. After taking a moment to compose himself, he exhales. "Have you ever known a boy to attend a community college for four years? And not obtain a degree? All he ever talks about is—" Mr. Ball clears his throat and produces a stunning impersonation of Tayton as he continues "—hockey *praccy* and winning the *ship*."

The voice makes me snort, and I receive an elbow from Erick for my outburst.

Lifting his chin, Mr. Ball continues, "Mr. Vrieswyk continues to delude himself by taking classes where he falsely believes he'll receive easy As. We offer no such system in the theater department."

If you guessed that the moment Mr. Ball said, "*Easy A*," my mind immediately went to the classic Emma Stone film — you are correct. My mind movies are instantly replaying the montage of her running out the battery on her singing birthday card with increasingly dedicated renditions of "Pocket Full of Sunshine." Eventually, my eyes notice the long, sexy fingers wiggling in front of them.

"Hey, partner. You in there?"

"Totally. Of course. I'm familiar with Tayton. He's a troublemaker, but I don't think he's capable of attempted murder." I posed as a student once when I was investigating a campus murder, but I don't need to mention that detail to the prof.

Props to the theater professor. His lunging gasp and porcelain pallor are a shoo-in for a Tony nomination. "Murder?"

For a man who referred to it as mundane only moments ago, I've got to say I'm loving this tableau.

"Mr. Nowak's mother has been hospitalized as a result of injuries sustained during a break-in.

Someone attacked her in her place of business." Detective Harper is as professional as ever.

The professor rises from his throne of a chair, steps around his desk, and extends his hand toward Erick. "Please give my condolences to Mr. Nowak. It would be difficult to lose a mother at any age. I do hope she pulls through."

For some reason, that simple phrase knifes deep into my heart and tears spring to the corners of my eyes. "I'll be in the car."

Turning on a dime, I flee the professor's office, but not before catching his closing remarks. "Mr. Nowak is a creative genius. He will certainly find inspiration from this tragedy."

If I wasn't such a grown-up gal, I would up-chuck right here in the hallway.

Erick catches up with me as I'm exiting the fine arts building.

"Hey, are you all right, Moon?"

"Sure. Yeah. Just caught me off guard with that mom comment, you know?"

He slips an arm around my shoulders and hugs me close as he kisses the top of my head. "I absolutely know. Losing a mother at any age is hard. Losing one at eleven is devastating. You held it together like a champ in there. Would you like to accompany me to the admin building and see if we can get a schedule for this Tayton character?"

Shrugging my shoulders, I blow a raspberry and frown. "I mean, sure, we're supposed to follow every lead, but I know this kid. Remember the case with the archaeology professor? That Tayton kid was in my class. He might be a superstar at hockey, but he's not smart enough to organize anything beyond hitting a little black disc with a big brown stick. Seriously. He's not our man."

Erick types some notes into the app on his phone as he bites his lip. "I trust your intuition, probably more than I should, but I'm not comfortable leaving any loose ends on this one. I hope you don't feel like that's not enough trust." His big blue eyes plead for mercy.

"Nonsense. You trust the exact right amount. Any more, and you'd be a pushover. Any less, and you'd be in danger of losing your husband-of-the-year nomination."

He chuckles and kisses my cheek while I dry my tears.

"I think you forgot to shave this morning, Harper."

Erick leans in, and his soft blue eyes envelop me. "I think it's a little early in the relationship to be complaining about kisses, Moon."

Shoot, he's got me there. "Touché. I'll take your kisses anyway I can get 'em, Harper."

Chuckling, he replies, "Now that's more like it."

Exhaling in defeat, I share my hunch. "Ten to one, Tayton is pumping iron somewhere."

I may have been the expert on where to locate the theater, but my boy Ricky is all about that weight room.

"The campus and the sheriff's station had an unspoken agreement. We provided the majority of their security, allowing them to redirect funds to important educational programs, while they allowed our deputies use of the sports facilities."

"Isn't that what they call payola?" My honest, upstanding husband slows the car and stares at me with simmering indignation.

"Hey, I was kidding. I'm sure it was a great trade-off. Just having you guys on campus, even if you were only lifting weights or shooting hoops, I'm sure it served as a great deterrent." And that's me trying to un-wedge my foot from my mouth.

He depresses the accelerator and appears to forgive my faux pas.

"The weight room is between the gymnasium and the locker rooms." He turns off the ignition and tosses me the keys. "I'll be back in a couple minutes. You can start the Jeep if you get cold."

The keys land squarely on the floormat of the passenger side.

I don't catch things. "I'm sorry. Did I miss a company meeting or perhaps a supervisory memo?"

He shrugs and gazes at me in genuine confusion.

"Is there some reason you assume I'm not coming *into* the weight room with you? I'm the one who can smell guilt a mile away."

A flash of jealousy sweeps across his features like a summer storm over a tiny Pacific island. My extra senses click into high, but I choose to let him dig his own way out.

"Oh, you're welcome to join me. It wasn't guilt I was worried about. I just thought you'd rather avoid the stinking testosterone mess of it all."

Pocketing the keys, I hop out of the vehicle and meet him on the driver's side. "Translation: I'd rather not have my new bride checking out a bunch of sweaty, jacked man-boys."

He blushes, looks at his feet, and shrugs. "You can't blame a guy for trying."

Hooking my arm through his, I tug him toward the row of double doors. "Don't worry, Harper. Those boys don't have what I'm looking for."

He holds the door for me as he chuckles. "Is that so?"

Painting my features in the portrait of innocence, I turn and gaze upward at his dashing eyes. "Yeah. I like my men a little on the smarter side. If Tayton is any indication of the IQ level of your average jock, I'm good."

Externally, he laughs with ease. My clairsentience picks up on a ripple of relief beneath the surface.

When we walk into the weight room, I almost regret my decision. The place smells like old vinyl, armpits, and feet. None of these things are good. However, I say *almost* regret because the gladiatorial display is worth holding my breath for.

Erick takes one look at me, and his broad shoulders sink ever so slightly. "Do you see that hockey player?"

Currently in the squat rack, grunting and sweating with the best of them, the unmistakable blond mullet of Tayton Vrieswyk jumps out at me like a possessed clown in a haunted house. "That's your guy right there."

Harper takes in the scene and bobs his head. "Hmmm, he's squatting about 450 pounds. The guy definitely doesn't skip leg day."

Boys. Never stop comparing their toys.

Snaking my way through the obstacle-laden weight room, I feel like a long-tailed cat in a room full of rocking chairs. I might look cool on the outside, but if I lose my focus for even a second—

My toe catches on a dumbbell, and I lurch forward and brace for impact. None comes.

"Thanks for the save, Harper."

He winks. "Every time, Moon. Every time."

A likely teammate spots the weight bar for our guy and chants, "All you, bro. You got this!"

Tayton grunts loudly as he racks the loaded weight bar. He steps toward the teammate and chest bumps him with the ferocity of two rams during the rut. "Yeah! That's how we get those Ws."

I had definitely forgotten what sheer joy this would be. "Hey, Tayton. Remember me?"

He flicks the "party in the back" portion of his mullet over his shoulder and puffs up his chest. "Look, I can't keep track of every puck bunny— Oh, dude! Darcy Brown, am I right?"

Looks like he *can* keep track. Lucky for me, he said my fake name first, reminding me of the undercover identity I used during my brief stint as an archaeology student. "Sure. How ya been?"

He flexes his pecs and gestures toward himself. "See for yourself, eh?"

"I can see you're in the middle of a set. So I'll get right to the point." Nothing reveals the truth like a direct assault. "Who hired you to smash the Emporium?"

Have you ever watched the air leak out of a sad little latex balloon? This is a lot like that, only way more satisfying. Hooray for psychic me. My barely-a-hunch is right on target.

"What? What are you talking about?" He

glances toward his teammate, but his bro scurries off to the dumbbell rack.

If only Tayton was as good at acting as he was at hockey. May as well continue making wild assumptions and see where they lead. "Look, dude, we both know you were involved. Ania Karina said the guys who smashed up her shop had hockey sticks. And you were lipping off to her son in your theater-tech class. Doesn't take a CPA to crunch those numbers. What were you doing there?"

His face is a mass of confusion. I have no idea whether he's struggling with the term CPA, the idea of deductive reasoning, or something else entirely. "This got something to do with archaeology?"

Glancing heavenward, I silently call on the spirit of my "more bees with honey" grandmother. "Tayton, you're a rockstar on the ice, but your grades don't even chart. Buying term papers and hiring tutors can't be part of your scholarship. How much did the person pay you, and what did they look like?"

I think the term is power-play. Maybe it's a full-court press? Either way, I've got him exactly where I want him.

His eyes dart left, right, and then up to Erick. "You brought the sheriff?"

I definitely don't have time. "Looks that way to you." Pretty sure I can use his assumption to my advantage. "The truth, Tayton. Maybe he'll go easy on you."

Tayton backs against the wall of mirrors and scans the room. "It was some chick. Doesn't go here. Older, you know? But her body was straight fire, right?"

"I wouldn't know, Tayton." Wow! I need to speed this up. "Auburn hair, loose curls, about my height?"

He rubs his chin and chuckles. "Hold up. She ghost your boy or somethin'?" He gestures to Erick.

The extent of this man-boy's world . . . The limits are mind-boggling. "The description. Yes or no, Tayton?"

"Yeah, that's her. Said her name was Freddie or something. I don't know. She gave us each 500 large."

If this were a cartoon, my head would explode. "She gave you $5,000?"

He looks at me as though *I'm* the idiot. "Chill. 500 bucks. You know?"

One of us knows. And it's certainly not him.

"And who knocked the owner into the table?"

His hands shoot up in the air. "Whoa. Whoa. We didn't flex on no one. The Hammer and me just busted the place up, and we hit it."

At this point, I'm beginning to understand that even he doesn't understand his own slang. So, I'll assume he hit the road. "And was this redhead that hired you — was she there?"

"I didn't see her. Didn't see no one. Smashed and ran."

"Three of you?"

Once again, he tilts his head and looks at me in amusement. "No. Two." Tayton cracks his knuckles. "I gotta do my drop set. We good?"

"Yeah. We're cool."

Erick has his phone out. Without a shadow of a doubt, I'm sure that he's already calling Paulsen. She may not be able to pin anything more than the vandalism on Tayton and whoever The Hammer is, but sharing the lead is the right thing to do.

On the way back to the vehicle, Erick's working hard to suppress his grin. "I didn't know you spoke muscle head."

"I don't think they even speak it. If it wasn't for my extra senses, I doubt I would've gotten anything out of that conversation. The woman he described could definitely be Artemis Ward, the chick that manipulated your fa— I mean, Alex Crenshaw. If it was her, and she's as dangerous as Silas suspects, that changes everything. We've got to—"

My phone rings, and I answer it on speakerphone as I close my door. "Hey, Tadjo. What can I do for you?"

"I wanted to let you know the hospital called."

His voice cracks. "She's regained consciousness, but still not talking. They told me to give her a few more hours before I visit." He draws a ragged breath. "Do you think you could get anything?"

I'm certain he's referring to my not-so-secret abilities, but I'll play dumb. "If she's uncommunicative, I'm not sure what I could uncover."

"I was hoping maybe you had a break in the case . . ." His voice lacks its usual flair.

"Nothing rock solid. I think we have to revisit the 'enemies' angle one more time. I know you only recently patched things up with your mother and are doing everything you can to care for her, but there has to be something we're missing."

"All the patrons who come into the shop love my matka. Maybe it's an online issue." His breathing quickens.

"Online?" This is the first I'm hearing of anything online, and I'm wondering if it's something he pushed his mother into. Maybe he didn't mention it because of a guilty conscience. "Tadjo, this might be the town that tech forgot, but if your mother was venturing into online potion sales . . . I think we all know what an unfriendly, troll-filled place the internet can be."

He sighs, and I can picture him gazing heavenward. "Critics are pure evil."

"I'll head over to the hospital and see if your

mom can give me a description of her attacker, or some clue as to what happened. Why don't you go through the online orders and look for anything unusual — anything that stands out? Especially if it was a local pick-up."

There's a pregnant pause that says he suspects something that he's not planning to share. I'll let it lie for now. Once I talk to Ania, I'm going to get to the bottom of that pause.

Tadjo inhales slowly. "Perhaps I was too hasty. I'll look through the online transactions." His voice shifts, and his tone belies a smile. "Tell my mother how strong she is. I know she can pull through. Between you, me, and the velvet curtain, I just can't do a funeral this time of year. Too depressing!"

I recognize a kindred spirit when I hear one. Tadjo has clearly chosen to hide his worry beneath a blanket of dark humor.

Laughing to support his efforts, I offer encouragement. "Don't get ahead of yourself. Your mother is a feisty woman."

"Don't I know it!" He laughs with panache and sighs. "I'll ring you if I find anything."

"Copy that."

Erick puts the vehicle in drive and stomps on the gas. He's never one to miss an opportunity to push the limits of the posted speed or the vehicle he's driving.

"Easy, *Speed Racer*. Once we get back to the office, I'm only going to abandon you."

His pouty mouth frowns. "We're not going to the hospital together?"

"Divide and conquer, my good man."

"10-4, *Caesar*."

"*Et tu, Brute?*"

CHAPTER 7

ACCORDING TO MY CALCULATIONS, taking witness statements qualifies as official PI hours. I'm kinda happy to leave Erick at the office to deal with a possible pop-in. I can't take another run-in with Bristol. Nothing against her. The fawning makes me uncomfortable. The best use of my skills will be heading over to the hospital to see if I can divine anything from the semi-conscious Mrs. Nowak.

All the dark clouds hanging in the sky have parted, and the first truly blue sky I've seen in months spreads over the sleepy town of Pin Cherry Harbor.

Back in Arizona, I'm sure temperatures are north of 80°F at this point. But I don't exactly miss it.

Before Silas Willoughby found me and enticed

me to venture farther north than I'd ever been in my life, I couldn't have imagined enjoying winter. Now that I have new traditions, like the Yuletide Extravaganza, the Lighthouse Festival, the Sled Dog Meet & Greet, and the Candlelight Ski Night, I wouldn't trade this life for anything.

The parking lot at the hospital is unusually empty. As the region's only trauma center, they typically get a lot of business from the surrounding towns and cities.

I'm not one to look a gift horse in the mouth, though. If this means that fewer people are suffering today, I'll take it. The gal at the front desk doesn't immediately recognize me, which surprises me a bit since my father and I are the only people in town with bone-white hair and what I'm told are dreamy grey eyes. However, once I mention my name, she smiles broadly. "Oh, Miss Moon. How have you been?"

"Good. And it's Mrs. Moon. Married, but I kept my maiden name."

Her pale-blue eyes twinkle as she leans forward. "Did you finally land that Ricky Harper?"

I'm not sure where this conversation is going, but I don't see a ready escape hatch. "We just celebrated our first anniversary last month."

She yanks her phone from the pocket of her scrubs, and her fingers fly over the keys as she talks to me. "The girls from my old homeroom will never believe this! Not sure if any of the bets still hold, but I was the one who insisted that Ricky would never marry a local!" She waves her hand to stave off any interruption. "I know you live here now, but technically you aren't a local." Her potential win has her glowing.

Having already had a longer conversation than I ever intended, I hope to take advantage of her distraction. "Can you tell me which room Mrs. Nowak is in?"

She temporarily sets her phone on the desk and taps some information into the computer. "She's on the second floor. She was moved out of intensive care about an hour ago. You'll have to check at the nurses' station to see if they're allowing visitors."

"Thanks for your help." Without a backward glance, I scurry toward the elevator and an elevated odor of disinfectants. Looks like I'll be having a little fun when I pick up my husband. I can't wait to ask Erick if he knew anything about this marriage pool.

The second-floor nurses' station is a flurry of activity. Despite the empty parking lot, these women seem pushed to the breaking point.

As I approach the desk, one of them glances toward me, and even without the aid of my psychic abilities, I can tell she's desperate for any port in a storm.

"I was going to ask you if Mrs. Nowak is accepting visitors, but is there something I can do for you?"

The petite blonde practically lunges over the counter. She grips my arm with both of her hands and pleads, "She's in room 222. If there's anything you can do to calm her—"

"I'm on it."

Joining the parade of nurses streaming up and down the hall, it's not hard to find the common origin point. They're all coming in and out of room 222, seemingly propelled by commands uttered in a thick Polish accent.

A tall brunette in purple scrubs dives from the room. I softly grab her arm. "Why don't you and all the nurses go get a cup of coffee? I've got Mrs. Nowak covered for at least the next fifteen minutes."

The woman bends and nearly lays her head on my shoulder. "You might be an actual saint."

The phrase tickles something in the back of my brain, but I don't have time to make the connection right now. I slip into room 222 and prepare for the worst. "Good afternoon, Mrs. Nowak. You've made a remarkable recovery."

The woman propped in the bed has a long grey

braid trailing over her shoulder and most of the way down her arm. In the past, I've only seen it carefully pinned around the circumference of her head. The scene Tadjo described this morning seems utterly unbelievable.

"Have you come to avenge me?"

At least, that's what I believe I heard. It takes a moment for me to reacquaint myself with her thick accent.

"Why don't you tell me what you remember, and then I'll decide if any avenging needs to be done."

She tugs at her covers, creases the fold in the sheet, and points to a rolling table barely an inch from her hand. "First a drink."

Seems like she expects me to wait on her in the absence of her army of nurses. No problem.

Picking up the salmon-pink container of ice and water, I tilt the straw toward her and lift the contraption to her lips.

She takes a scant sip, pushes the pink cup away, and exhales in disgust. "I prefer my well water. No chemicals."

"Yes, I'm sure your well water is better. Now tell me about this morning."

"You are not like your grandmother." The faint tinge of admiration in her gaze is the only indication that her words are meant as a compliment.

If she's attempting to bait me into an argument, I'm not biting. "My grandmother has changed since her time in Pin Cherry."

Ania Karina frowns. "Perhaps these afterlife trials and tribulations . . . they help her?"

If this woman expects me to thank her for what she put me through when she trapped Grams' ghost in an amulet— "Will you please tell me what happened yesterday morning?"

"No tricks? You have no spell?" She leans away and eyes me warily.

"Mrs. Nowak, I am not a witch. No spells to cast. I believe people should be allowed to choose their own actions. Will you help me? I hope you'll find it in your heart to do so." Lifting both hands, I show her my palms. "No tricks."

She sighs with satisfaction. "I was in the back room." Ania pauses and waits for me to give an indication of understanding. I may not be a regular at Ania's Emporium, but she knows I've been there a handful of times. Regardless, she appears to have no intention of continuing until I confirm.

"Yes, behind the beaded curtain. Please continue."

"Out front, the bell rings. I am an old woman. With cane."

I have a very specific question about her cane, which I suspect is secretly a powerful staff imbued with magical properties, but I'll hold that question. "Yes, I've seen your cane."

She makes a sound somewhere between a scoff and one of Silas Willoughby's harrumphs. "When I come into the store, there is smashing and shouting. Unholy vandals."

"Vandals? So, there was definitely more than one person?"

Ania Karina narrows her gaze, but nods firmly. "Yes. Three. This is what I say." She shakes her head and continues, "I tell them to leave, or I call police."

"What did they do?"

"The one with no stick keeps rummaging through my things."

"One didn't have a stick? Who had sticks?"

"Yes. The two smashers had sticks for hockey. I tell you this before."

She told me no such thing, but I'll let it slide.

"So I lift my cane, and I—" She stops, and I can sense her struggling with whether to tell me the truth.

"You were going to cast a spell?"

She nods brusquely. "But I cannot speak. So, nothing happens. The one with no stick shoves me. I fall and hit my head on walnut table."

"I'm very sorry that happened to you, Mrs.

Nowak. Can you describe the one who shoved you — or any of the vandals?"

Once again, she fusses with her blankets and narrows her gaze. "They all wear masks. The hooded sweatshirts and hockey masks."

Definitely sounds like Tayton and his crew, although he swore there were only two of them. Maybe Artemis was the one without the stick, or maybe she came in after the— But Tayton said he never saw her. Silas once taught me an alchemical working to create temporary invisibility . . . Could Artemis have been walking right past Tayton without him knowing?

"Did you see — Did they take anything?"

The woman tugs angrily at her sheet and levels a gaze that would likely turn mere mortals into pillars of salt. "How do I know this? I have the blackout. I tell you. My head. Hit on the table." She's gesticulating wildly, and I know my next statement won't calm her.

"It's all right. Tadjo went through the inventory." Probably best if I don't mention my participation in that little venture. "He said the only thing missing is the Eye of the Priestess."

Mrs. Nowak gasps as though it could be her last breath and clutches her chest with a gnarled hand. "No. Not the Eye!"

Continuing with the theme of keeping my cards

close to the vest, I attempt to draw out more. "Can you tell me about the Eye of the Priestess?"

"Great power." She clutches her blanket in both hands and twists it back and forth. "More curse than blessing."

"Who thought it was a blessing?"

"The priestess, you foolish girl."

I'll ignore that last part. "You have some first-hand knowledge of the priestess who fashioned the thing?"

"The Eye is ancient. It was made by no mortal. The goddess Isis, she makes this gift of the Eye to the woman who defends her shrine."

"And this woman who defended the shrine, she was a priestess who lost an eye?"

This time, she scoffs openly. "So, some wisdom has dripped down from that fossil of a demon you call a mentor."

"Easy does it, Mrs. Nowak. Silas Willoughby is no demon. I know you haven't seen eye to eye on things in the past, but he's your only hope of recovering this relic."

"Not if the intruder has the incantation."

Luckily, I don't have to *play* dumb. "Incantation? Where would she find this incantation?"

Mrs. Nowak crosses her arms over her sagging bosom, clamps her jaw, and shakes her head. The motion causes immediate pain, and she presses a gnarled hand to her temple.

"Ania, people could die. It's possible that the woman who stole the eye is a powerful sorceress. If it's the person I suspect, she's responsible for manipulating someone into killing two people already. You're lucky to be alive."

Mrs. Nowak spits over her left shoulder, but slowly uncrosses her arms. "No. Not luck. I have protections in my Emporium."

I remember Silas battling against those protections on at least one of our previous encounters. Best not to remind her. "Then I'm glad that your protections were in place. But we don't know who or what she's after. Her next target may not be as prepared as you. I need to know the incantation."

Her mouth moves soundlessly, and I'm not sure if she's literally chewing on her answer or mumbling a spell.

Lucky for me, it was the former.

"How is my sweet boy?" An unusual warmth lingers on her face, and for a moment, I'm utterly distracted.

"Tadjo? He's fine. He's worried sick about you. He'll be so happy to hear that you're able to carry on a conversation."

She locks eyes with me, and for a few seconds I see the young, powerful gypsy witch vibrantly thrumming inside her. "Tell him to give you the grimoire."

"Your grimoire? Are you sure?"

Once again, she stares into my eyes, and I feel her burrowing into my soul. "I have no daughter. She was lost to me in childbirth." Sudden tears well in the corner of her eyes.

"You had a daughter?" I place my hand on her crooked fingers. Pyewacket! That toy baby bottle . . . Once again, my fiendish feline is a step ahead.

"She came after my precious Tadjo. I named her Annie Spuścizna, but she had no breath."

Maybe there is something worse than losing a mother. The thought of a stillborn child makes my heart ache inside my chest. "I'm so sorry, Mrs. Nowak. Did they let you hold her?"

Ania Karina's chest heaves as she clutches her hospital gown. "Different times. The nurse, she took her. I see only a birthmark on her neck. A broken crescent moon. A bad omen."

I'd never heard anyone refer to the moon as a bad omen, but I'm no expert. I have to change the subject. The old woman is struggling to breathe. This horrible memory certainly can't be good for Mrs. Nowak's recovery.

"Maybe you can give the grimoire to Tadjo. I know he takes good care of your shop, Mrs. Nowak."

She shakes her head vigorously, and her braid whips back and forth as misery twists her features. "He must give it to you. I see it now. You are the spuścizna. The legacy." Once again, Mrs. Nowak presses a hand to the bandage at her temple as her breathing becomes labored and shallow.

Salty drops spill from my own eyes, and I lean forward to embrace the woman who was once my grandmother's most dangerous rival. "Thank you, Ania. I won't let you down. I'll protect your family. I promise."

As I release her from my grasp, her grey-shrouded head falls forward.

The machine to my left emits one agonizing, endless wail.

Two nurses race into the room as I step back to let them check on Mrs. Nowak.

One calls a code blue.

I attempt to make myself small as the room fills with medical personnel. A young female doctor calls out orders, and the nurses work in flawless unison. Something is injected into Mrs. Nowak's IV line, and the doctor calls for paddles.

They shock Mrs. Nowak three times, and mentally I applaud their valiant efforts. However, in my heart of psychic hearts, I know she's truly gone. There will be no miraculous recovery this time.

Eventually, fate comes for us all.

CHAPTER 8

DRIVING TOWARD THE EMPORIUM, my head is in a daze. I have no idea what I'm going to say to Tadjo, but I know I have to do it in person.

Gripping the cold metal handle, I take a deep breath and push into the shop, accompanied by the mystical tinkle of the replaced chimes.

"Oh! Mitzy, I thought you'd never get back here." Tadjo must have overheated while he searched through the online store records. He's removed his scarf and his slouchy beanie is pushed back from his forehead, revealing close-cropped, shockingly grey hair.

"Tadjo, there's something—"

"I think I found what we're looking for!"

He waves a piece of paper wildly and hurries toward me.

My eyes instinctively scan the type. "So this Sheila Frenet woman bought a curse to use against her neighbor? A neighbor she suspected of attempting to poison her dogs?"

Tadjo nods eagerly. "Yes! And then she was furious when it didn't work!"

Scanning the sheet for the follow-up complaint, I have to admit even a seasoned amateur sleuth like myself is shocked. "Listen to this. 'You're a fraud and a profiteer! I'm going to make sure you never sell another fake potion as long as you live. However short that might be!'" Tadjo and I exchange a headshake. "That sounds like a definite threat."

He snatches the paper from my hand, scans the printed email message as though he's only seeing it for the first time, and continues to nod. "You should definitely talk to this woman. Most definitely. Sounds exactly like the type of person who would smash their way through the shop to make a point. If her intention was to put my mother out of busine — OMG! Maybe her intention was to injure my mother all along!"

Tadjo's words remind me of the horrible news I have to share. Taking a deep breath, I get directly to the point.

He weeps when he learns of his mother's passing, but he's grateful she was not alone.

When I relate the details of her final wishes regarding the grimoire, I expect resistance.

He exhales slowly and draws a ragged breath. "I'm not one-tenth of the magic wielder my mother was, but I sensed a connection to you the first time we spoke on the phone. I wasn't between shows in New York like I said. Truth is, I was in the middle of directing the greatest comeback show in history, but I felt there was a higher calling. If I failed to come back to Pin Cherry Harbor, I knew I would regret it for the rest of my life."

I try to thank him, but my tears are flowing heavily now, and my voice is just a garbled sob. After a couple attempts to catch my breath, I offer my condolences. "If you ever want to talk about your mother's passing, I'm here for you. Also, I'm sorry about your sister."

Tadjo tugs his beanie forward and gazes at me with suspicious confusion. "I don't have a sister."

Oops. Leave it to me to spill another family secret. "Your mother never told you about the baby she lost? She said Annie would've been younger than you. Maybe you were too little to remember."

His gaze drifts away and suddenly snaps back. "The summer she went to my babcia's! Ray is five years older than me. I bet he knows some— Oh! Raymond. I should call my brother."

"Of course. You can bring the grimoire to the

bookstore tomorrow." As I lean in to hug Tadjo one more time, he throws his hands in the air and shouts.

"That's where I've seen it!"

"Are you talking about the grimoire? You've seen something about the missing item in your mother's grimoire?" I'm an obsessive watcher of film and television. If anyone knows the importance of an ancient family grimoire — it's me.

Tadjo nods guiltily. "I thought of the Eye of the Priestess being in the grimoire earlier, but I didn't want to tell you."

"Um, I have to see that. If your mother had notes about this Eye of the Priestess in that book . . . It would really help us out. I don't need to remove it from the premises or anything right now. But I definitely need to look at it."

When he leaves to fetch the book from the back room, I place a quick call to Silas. Not on speakerphone.

"Silas, I only have a minute. That missing item from the shop — the Eye of the Priestess — Tadjo is getting Ania's grimoire right now. He's certain there's something in there. I'll read everything I can and get back to you."

The hesitant tone in my mentor's voice as he quietly agrees concerns me more than anything else we've encountered today.

Ending the call, I slip the phone into my back pocket as Tadjo returns. He clears a space on the one table that remains upright and reverently lays the book on the thick walnut surface. "Please be careful. It's the only link I have to our history." Another actual tear leaks from the corner of his eye.

"I'll be careful. I promise." Gently opening the sacred book, I leaf through the pages until the tingling hairs on the back of my neck indicate I've reached the information I need.

On the left is a hand-drawn image. An ebony black sphere enrobed by gold. The iris appears to be lapis lazuli, and the pupil could be a black diamond or onyx. My clairsentience gets a hit. Definitely onyx. It's beautiful and terrifying to behold.

"What does it say on the right?" Tadjo steps closer, but I hold up my hand to keep him at bay. Pulling the phone from my pocket, I take a photo of each page and close the book without saying a word.

Tadjo groans with concern. "What is it?"

"Is there somewhere safe — like impenetrable — that you can keep this book?"

He shakes his head, and fear tightens the muscles around his eyes. "Is it serious?"

"Deathly." Swallowing hard, I glance toward his worried face and hope my plea reaches him. "I need to take this book to Silas Willoughby. He — he will know how to protect this information. If the person who stole the eye gets hold of this book—"

Tadjo steps forward and grips my hands. "I trust you, Mitzy. Take it."

As I reach for the book, he steps forward and grabs my hand again. "Wait. There's a special pouch." He disappears into the back room and returns with a black leather satchel. Tadjo slips his mother's tome inside, twists the cord around a deer horn button, and hands it to me. "If there's anything I can do to help, you'll tell me, right?"

"I will."

Time to pick up my husband and inform him that our *pre*-murder investigation has taken a deadly turn.

CHAPTER 9

As I PULL into the parking lot at Harper and Moon Investigations, a wave of sadness hits me like a tsunami. Tears pour from my eyes. My heart feels as though it's being torn from my chest.

All of this has more to do with losing my mother when I was eleven than the passing of Ania Karina Nowak. The thread that connects the two is, of course, losing a mother. Tadjo and his brother Ray are grown men. Their mother was advanced in age and unwell. No one is truly prepared for death, but they definitely had time to make their peace with it.

But a preteen and her babysitter, interrupted by a knock on the door, revealing terrible news regarding her sole parent's sudden and tragic death — there's no comparison. Silas always tells me I must speak the names of the dead lest they be forgotten. "Mama . . . Coraline Moon, I didn't have enough time with you. You were the best mother any girl could have ever had. I'm not sure why you chose to raise me on your own, but I'm happy to tell you I found my father. I reconnected with Jacob, and together we're building a life that would make you proud."

A knock on the car window nearly separates my soul from my body.

"Holy horror movie, Batman!"

Erick opens my door, takes one look at my face, and swallows me in a tender yet comforting hug. "What happened? Are you okay?"

"Yeah. I'm totally fine. I just happened to be at the hospital when Mrs. Nowak crossed over. It brought up—"

He pulls me from the car, tightens his embrace, and kisses the top of my head. "You don't have to say. I know how much you miss your mother. I'm sorry I never had the chance to meet her. Any woman responsible for raising the amazing Mitzy Moon had to have been a force to be reckoned with."

I have no idea how he always knows the right thing to say, but he does. My tears slacken, and I push onto my tiptoes to kiss his sweet, pouty mouth.

As I pull away, the worries over the grimoire flood in.

"What else?" Erick narrows his gaze.

"Are you trying to steal my thing? I'm the one with hunches, Harper."

When I look at Erick, I see the deep concern darkening his gaze.

"How bad is it, Moon?"

"We need to take Ania Karina's grimoire directly to Silas. Now."

Erick swallows, and the muscles in his jaw clench. He walks me to the opposite side of my Jeep and opens the passenger door. I climb in without resistance.

He hops in the driver's seat and holds out his hand. "Keys?"

Pointing to the ignition, I offer a weak grin. "I'm here, in the passenger seat. No argument from me. It's definitely best for you to drive . . . I'm a mess."

"I got you, Moon." He gently takes the keys. "Thanks."

Whoever stole this magical item is powerful. They knew what they were looking for . . . This definitely wasn't as random as it was made to seem.

One name shimmers in the ether.

Artemis Ward.

My mind replays Erick's report on the things

Alex Crenshaw told him when Erick visited the state penitentiary three months ago. Alex wasn't sure whom Artemis Ward was coming after, but he knew she wouldn't stop until she got what she was looking for. Maybe all she wanted was this artifact. Now that she has the Eye of the Priestess, maybe she'll leave Pin Cherry Harbor.

My heart wishes that were true; my head knows different.

Erick fishtails out of the parking lot, and we drive to Silas Willoughby's remote Gothic mansion in tense silence.

As we wind down Mr. Willoughby's tree-lined drive, my eye catches a break in the black-and-white birch. "Turn here."

My chauffeur slows as his expression shifts from doubt to surprise. "Whoa, I didn't even see that turn. Weird."

Years ago, I never would've explained. "You can't see it. Only people like me and Silas can see the turn."

He nods and glances at me from the corner of his eye. "So what you're saying is I'm not special, is that right?"

"Oh brother. That's not what I'm saying at all. You're very special, Ricky. Now park in front of that first garage, and let's get this book inside."

Before I make it two steps from the Jeep, Silas is shuffling out his back door toward me. "Is it safe?"

His level of concern should make me nervous, but I never deal with stress like a normal person. Dark humor is what comforts me.

"Don't you mean, 'Is it secret? Is it safe?', Gandalf?"

Silas pauses, considers my words, and, in spite of the situation, chuckles. "I have come to relish your twisted japery, Mizithra."

Classic Silas. "Good to hear. Because you won't be laughing for the next hundred years after you read this little passage about the Eye of the Priestess."

Silas takes the black satchel from me, and our small parade hurries toward his library. "How is it that you convinced Mrs. Nowak to allow the book to leave her shop?"

"Unfortunately, she crossed over earlier today as a result of her injuries."

"May Light support her spirit. So mote it be." Silas breathes a deep sigh. "That must have been difficult for you."

"Yeah. It was a tough moment. Brought up a lot of stuff for me."

A long silence lies between us. "You must miss your mother terribly."

"I do. I also understand how losing her so young

and struggling through foster care gave me the ability to appreciate what I have now — a whole lot more. Never thought I'd hear myself say that."

"You are demonstrating growth. When the student is ready, the teacher arrives. Without the events that shaped your life, you may never have discovered Pin Cherry Harbor."

"I'm sure you're right about that. Anyway, Mrs. Nowak left me her grimoire. It was her final wish. So, I guess you can just add that to my training, or whatever."

Silas harrumphs. "Unacceptable. It is not my intention to blur the lines between magic and alchemy with regard to your training."

"Copy that."

"And on the matter of alchemy, I am working on several things that will distract and redirect Artemis Ward. I aim to force her down a difficult path as she continues her search for the incantation."

His library flooring is an intricate marble design, and the stack of books that normally cover the sturdy oak table has been partially cleared to make room for my offering.

Silas carefully removes the sacred book from the satchel, and I step forward to show him the page, referencing the missing relic.

"This is the item that was taken." I point toward

the gilded eye.

Silas grumbles deeply as he scans across the right-hand page of script.

He turns toward me and grips with my shoulders. "I pray you did not read this aloud."

"No. I scanned it over and— Hey, I *have* learned a few things from you."

He breathes a sigh of relief and pats my shoulder. "I am thankful for that."

Erick steps forward and grins sheepishly. "Look, I know I'm kind of on the outside here, but could somebody get me up to speed?"

Silas nods as he exhales. "Yes. Of course. The item, which we postulate is now in the possession of Artemis Ward, is powerful indeed. The Eye of the Priestess is exactly as it appears. A potent Egyptian priestess who served Isis, either lost an eye or had one purposely removed. She then wrought this enchanted talisman." He points toward the left-hand page. "This ornate prosthetic replaced her sacrificed human eye."

Erick shrugs. "Doesn't sound so bad. It's basically a piece of jewelry. A placeholder, right?"

Silas smooths his mustache with a thumb and forefinger as he shakes his head. "If only it were that innocuous. The prosthetic eye was imbued with powers beyond imagination. How Ania Karina Nowak came to possess the incantation described here we may never know. What we do know is that this incantation, if spoken aloud, will reactivate the Eye of the Priestess."

To my husband's credit, he's nodding as though he truly believes in all these supernatural shenanigans.

"If the eye is reactivated, it will allow anyone who possesses it to penetrate the veil of the supernatural. The spell becomes a curse to all who oppose the priestess. It will allow the priestess to uncover the true nature behind any spell or alchemical working as long as she is in possession of the Eye." Silas shakes his head, and his jowls seem to sag an additional measure.

Little sparks of understanding are lighting in Erick's eyes. Time for me to step in.

I blow the flames to life. "So, whatever Silas has done to hide himself from discovery would be revealed. And you know what she did to the other members of the secret society."

Erick's deep-blue eyes darken. "We still can't be sure she was responsible for any of that. Alex Crenshaw is sitting in prison for those two murders, and I'm not entirely certain the wrong man was locked up."

"Well, I am. I know she manipulated him. Maybe there was a part of him that went along with her, and for that, I guess he got what he deserved.

But Artemis Ward is dangerous. We can't let her find Silas. She would dispense with him and absorb his knowledge without hesitation. Artemis would become unstoppable." A full-body shudder rocks over me.

Off to the side, Silas runs his finger over the illustration of the Eye of the Priestess and mumbles, "The Queen shall protect the King."

The fact that each member of the secret society represented a different chess piece had little meaning to me. However, now that the Bishop, the Knight, and the Rook have been taken out. I'm far more concerned about the board-game analogy.

"Silas, you never told me about the King. Who are you protecting?"

His rheumy eyes clear, and he straightens to his impressive full stature. "Some things are not meant to be known."

With that, he steps toward a life-sized marble statue of Hermes Trismegistus, according to the placard, and presses on the great toe of the left foot. He whispers an incantation followed by a series of sigils drawn in the air. With a whoosh, a section of his mahogany bookcase slides back, and his secret vault rolls open.

Erick inhales sharply and steps backward. I feel the intense thickening of the air around us. If I were to attempt to move toward the vault, I could not.

My expanded psychic abilities are able to sense far more of the subtle workings in place than the previous time I witnessed the vault being opened.

Silas places the black satchel inside, reverses the order of the sigils, and again whispers an incantation.

In the past, he was more careful about hiding these things from me. He knows my extrasensory perception and my psychic recall will allow me to perform the incantations. Why would he purposely let me hear them? Unless . . .

"Silas! Nothing is going to happen to you, right?"

"My dear Mizithra, none of us is promised tomorrow. This is one of the reasons I encourage you to live in the here and now. Each day is precious. Remember that."

My chest tightens as I step forward and throw my arms around his neck. Crushing my face against his fusty tweed coat, I whisper, "Please tell me you're not planning anything foolish?"

He pats my back and steps out of my embrace. "I believe you've known me long enough to understand nothing I attempt is foolish."

Classic Silas non-answer.

"So, what's our next move?"

Silas turns, and raw power rages in his eyes. "*We* have no move. You and Erick will return to the bookshop. Do not remove the key or your mother's necklace until I tell you it is safe." He pauses. "Do you still have the quartz pendant I gave you for communicating?"

"Yes. Why?" I clutch the faceted crystal rod, grouped with the growing collection of necklaces beneath my shirt.

"I shall send word once your safety has been secured."

He's waiting for me to respond, but my loyal heart can't accept doing nothing. It may not be the right choice, but my foster brother Jarrell loved to use the phrase, "it's always easier to ask for forgiveness than permission." Of course, that little lecture generally preceded him teaching me a new grift to run on unsuspecting townsfolk. If I ever run into that guy, I'm not sure whether I'll thank him or punch him in the gut. He led me down a darker path than I probably would've taken on my own, but a lot of the stuff he taught me has kept me alive in some sticky situations. Maybe Jarrell was a guardian angel in disguise. Hard to believe.

"Mizithra, are you having a vision?" He moves toward me with concern.

Oops! Lost in my mind movies and missing out on real life. "No. Nothing useful."

Silas harrumphs with more gusto than usual. "I recommend you send Twiggy on a book collection journey. The bookshop must remain closed until I have dealt with Artemis Ward." The tone of his deep voice has a ring of finality that even a snoopy rule breaker like me knows better than to challenge.

"Copy that."

CHAPTER 10

"YOU BETTER DRIVE US HOME, HARPER." There
are no tears left for me to cry today, but my brain is
spinning out of control with ways to secretly defy
my over-protective mentor.

He glances across the console and arches one
eyebrow. "Home? Am I hearing you correctly,
Moon?"

"Right. Sorry, I'm not thinking straight. I know
Silas is going to do something dangerous. I can't
bear to think of him doing that alone."

Erick adjusts his hands on the steering wheel
and mumbles.

"I didn't quite catch that, mumbler. Care to repeat it for the cheap seats?"

He chuckles. "I said, I assumed you wouldn't
take this lying down."

"Good. So we're on the same page. Let's figure out where Artemis Ward is holed up and come up with some kind of strategy to foil her plan."

"Gee, Brain, what are we gonna do tonight?" Erick snickers.

If he thinks for one minute that he can out TV trivia me, he's sadly mistaken. "The same thing we do every night, Pinky . . . try to take over the world!"

After an appropriate bow to my superior TV knowledge, Erick gets us back on track. "Did you happen to hear anyone mention Mrs. Nowak's cause of death?" he asks as he fires up the Jeep.

"I'm sure the claim will be some complication from what happened at her shop. Maybe internal bleeding from a cerebral hemorrhage . . . But I was there, Erick. I felt her choose to go."

He pulls into the garage, tosses the keys under the visor, and exhales slowly. "I had a buddy go like that. In the field. It was an ambush in Afghanistan. Heavy fire. He was hit two or three times. But, with modern medicine, he could've made it. He squeezed my hand and whispered a message for his mother." Erick's gaze drifts to a faraway place. The place where he keeps all his pain under lock and key.

"Did you give her the message?"

Erick nods, but makes no effort to speak.

I can sense how close the emotions are to the

surface. If he opens his mouth, too much will spill out. Reaching over the console, I squeeze his knee and nod my head. "You were a good friend."

His large hand grips mine and squeezes so hard I feel my bones might crack. There's no power on earth that will allow me to utter a single sound. This isn't a moment I dare interrupt.

Several minutes pass, and my severe lack of patience is taking its toll. Thankfully, Erick breaks the silence.

"We should go update the murder board and the rest of the team." A deep sadness tinges his gruff voice.

"Yep. We should totally do that."

We exit the vehicle, enter through the alleyway door, and stomp the snow off our boots.

Upstairs in my old apartment, we've assembled the whole gang.

Pyewacket has little interest, and is lounging on the antique four-poster bed with his eyes firmly closed.

Grams floats high above us, gazing through the 6 x 6, slumped-glass windows at the moon peeking over the horizon and reflecting on the snow-covered lake.

"She said that? She actually gave you her grimoire?"

Embracing my job as an afterlife interpreter, I

repeat Ghost-ma's question for Erick's benefit be-fore answering. "Yeah. Well, she wanted Tadjo to give it to me. She said she lost her only daughter in childbirth, and she knew I was the legacy. What legacy is she talking about?"

Grams floats downward like a feather on the wind. "You'll have to ask Silas, dear. Ania and I were never close — as you well know."

Now is definitely not the time to bring up the lifelong rivalry and the underhanded maneuvers on both sides of the battle. "All right. But what's our next move? We have no idea where to find Artemis Ward, and we have to make sure she doesn't get—"

"Mitzy! That's brilliant!"

My face scrunches in confusion. "What's bril-liant? I didn't say anything."

Erick seems to unknowingly be on the same wavelength as my resident ghost as he asks, "We don't know where Artemis Ward is, but we know what she wants. She wants that incantation, right?"

"Well, sure. She's always a step ahead of us, so she must know there's a way to activate the Eye of the Priestess."

Grams zooms toward me, stopping mere inches from my face. Her ghostly glow seems to have turned up its wattage. "Yes. She'll want to find the incantation. If you go undercover at the Emporium—"

Leaping from the settee, I pass directly through my grandmother's apparition. The warm hum of her energy temporarily distracts me. "Um, hold on. You want me to use myself as bait?"

Erick tilts his head and raises a hand. "Hey, I'm only hearing one side of this, but I don't like the word bait — unless you're talking about sunfish or perch."

I giggle and shrug.

Eager to argue her case, Grams rushes toward him and goosebumps immediately rise on his flesh.

I've never gotten them, since I've always been able to see and hear Ghost-ma. "Myrtle Isadora! Give the boy some room. You're scaring him."

She quickly backs away. "Sorry! Tell him how sorry I am, sweetie."

"Grams apologizes."

Erick dips his head in that endearing way that insinuates he's doffing a cap. "No big deal. I'm actually starting to get used to it."

"So, Grams wasn't saying bait, exactly. She wants me to go undercover at the Emporium."

He presses into the scalloped-back chair generally reserved for my mentor. "Okay. I like undercover better than bait. What exactly are you going to do if Artemis shows up?"

Grams darts forward, but I raise a hand. "Give us a minute, Isadora."

She taps one finger on her perfectly lined lips and pulses with impatience.

Addressing my husband, I toss out some options. "I could go undercover as a goth chick. Pale makeup on my face, black lipstick . . . maybe a black wig and kind of spooky, dark clothing. That should make me fairly unrecognizable."

Erick shrugs and then crosses his arms in that yummy way that makes his biceps bulge. "Great. So you're undercover and you think you will be unrecognizable. Let's play out the scenario. Artemis Ward walks into the Emporium. Then what happens?"

"I would ignore her. Because goth chicks don't trip over themselves to help customers."

Ghost-ma claps her hands wildly. "Exactly. You're already in character!"

"Grams loves that so far. Anyway, eventually she'll ask me to help her find something. I'll be terrible at it, but maybe I can convince her to buy something. Then, if she uses a credit card, you could trace it."

The patient former sheriff shakes his head as he leans forward and places his elbows on his knees. "I'm not sure what that will buy you, Moon. The best you can hope for is finding the mailing address where the bills for the credit card are sent. Assuming it's even legitimate. Something tells me a criminal mastermind like Artemis Ward isn't rolling with her own credit cards."

It makes me crazy when he's so right. "Fine. I'm just getting started. Maybe there's a phone number attached to— Never mind. Same problem."

Myrtle Isadora freeze frames, and her ghostly image jumps like the misaligned tracking on an old VHS tape.

"Grams, what is it?"

"Number . . . Get her phone number! Tell her you'll ask the owner, and if you find what she's looking for, you'll give her a call. You can ping her tower or triangulate something — right?"

Her eager smile gives me the first twinge of hope I've had since Mrs. Nowak passed.

"Erick, Grams actually has a great idea. If I can get Artemis to give me her phone number, promising to call her if we find what she's looking for, could we track her somehow?"

He leans back with a grin and runs his thumb along his jawline. "Maybe. I might be able to get one of the deputies to help me. I'm still on pretty good terms with everybody."

My eyes roll of their own accord. "Except Paulsen."

Erick chuckles and shrugs. "Well, except that."

"Great. We have a plan. Let me call Tadjo and make sure it's all right with him."

Without my even asking, Grams swooshes into the giant walk-in closet I call *Sex and the City* meets *Confessions of a Shopaholic* to work on my undercover wardrobe.

Tadjo Nowak is instantly on board with the idea. He even has notes for my character. Yeesh. Perhaps an undercover gig with a frustrated Broadway director wasn't my best idea.

When the call ends, I head toward the closet.

"Hey, wife-y?"

Turning, I place one fist on my curvy hip and attempt a stern look. "Yes, Ricky?"

He grins. "You better let Silas know what's going on."

"He told me not to communicate with him. Silas has the grimoire for safekeeping and he's working on his end of things. I'll get in touch with him after my mission is successful."

Erick chews the inside of his cheek. "In other words, he can't stop you if he doesn't know?"

"Exactly. I can be a very sneaky little hobbitses."

My husband rises from the settee and exhales loudly. "I'm familiar."

"Where are you headed, Harper?" Suddenly,

the last thing I want is to be left alone in the book-store apartment.

"Meet you in the big bed in ten?" His eyebrows flash in spite of the exhausted droop of his shoulders.

"Deal."

CHAPTER 11

WHEN WHISKERS TICKLE MY CHEEK, I'm surprised to find Pyewacket slinking around the walk-up. Proving once again that this cat either has the power to pass through solid objects or has a warren of secret passages throughout my bookshop. "Let me guess, you'd like some breakfast?"

Rather than his usual vocal confirmation, Pyewacket darts down the stairs, vanishing in a blur of tan fur.

"Was it my breath?"

Silence.

The spot beside me is already empty, and the hint of caffeinated aroma wafting up the stairs confirms my suspicion that Erick Harper, early riser that he is, is already downstairs.

Tugging a thick robe around myself and shoving

my feet into slippers, I trudge down to the open-plan kitchen with the single-minded dream of coffee.

Husband-of-the-year candidate Erick Harper waits at the bottom of the stairs with a steaming mug of black gold.

"That's one step closer to the trophy, hubby."

He grins and flashes his eyebrows.

Stopping on the bottom step, my eyes dart left and right.

"Do you hear something?" Tilting my head like a confused pooch, I glance at Erick and receive no confirmation.

He shrugs. "Maybe it's your psychic thing. What does it sound like?"

Heading for the door that leads from our walkup into the bookshop, I call over my shoulder, "Music. Sounds like music. We both know there's no way Twiggy came in after I sent her on a book collection trip." Doubt creeps in. "Is there?"

Opening the door, I'm not surprised when it doesn't close behind me.

If there's trouble afoot, my brave partner refuses to let me face it alone.

Together, we creep across the first floor of the bookshop. As we move between the stacks, I momentarily lose focus and inhale the scent of literary worlds to be explored.

Mentally smacking myself on the forehead, I get back on task and reach out with my extrasensory feelers.

Confirmed. My volunteer employee, Twiggy, is not here.

I whisper to my co-conspirator, "Not the back room. Sounds like it's coming from my old apartment."

Erick nods and makes a series of hand signals — which I do *not* understand.

The simplest thing is to hang back and let Detective Too-Hot-To-Handle take the lead.

He leaps over the "No Admittance" chain at the foot of the wrought-iron circular staircase as though he's part panther. Luckily, he turns and helps me over the same, but I feel like my version is more "part hippopotamus."

At least I didn't have to attempt the chain on my own. Something that most certainly would've ended with a classic trip and fall. Just one of the hilarious mishaps that Twiggy accepts as a form of payment.

Yes, I'm clumsy. And apparently, her long-standing friendship with my not-as-dearly-departed-as-everyone-thinks grandmother and the amusing antics that make up my life are payment enough to keep her on staff.

A truly fortunate set of events. I know exactly

zero about running a bookshop, despite the years I've owned one.

When we reach the Rare Books Loft, Erick nods once.

I have to assume the nod is confirmation that he hears what I hear and plans to continue toward the apartment.

He then gestures for me to take the route down the outside of the right-hand row of carefully aligned oak reading desks — each with their brass lamp.

When I reach the bookshelves curving against the back of the mezzanine, he raises a hand for me to stay put.

I wish I could say I don't understand, but even a civilian like me knows what "Stop in the Name of Love" looks like.

He pulls the cleverly hidden lever, made to look like a candle sconce, and presses his back to the stationary wall as the bookcase door slides open.

The volume of the music increases immediately.

He crouches and peers around the corner.

Before I can whisper my question or make up a hand signal that might mean, "What do you see?" former Sheriff Erick Harper leans forward on one knee and laughs out loud. "Pyewacket? Are you a DJ?" He shakes his head and continues to chuckle.

That's all I can take. Storming into the apartment, I kick out one hip as I glance at my demon-spawn caracal attempting to sit innocently in front of the computer that is supposed to be reserved for emergency videoconferencing calls.

"You got a side hustle you need to tell me about, son?"

Pyewacket sniffs sharply and hits the mouse with one paw. The volume of the song increases.

"Why you little—"

Grams floats out of the closet, singing along, and seems genuinely surprised to see Erick and me in the apartment. "Well, good morning, sweetie."

"Good morning? What the heck is going on over here? Did you guys decide to open some sort of coffeehouse?" Stepping closer to the computer, I confirm what was tickling the back of my mind. The song Pye had been blasting is from one of the movies on my all-time favorites list, *O Brother, Where Art Thou?*

Grams giggles absently. "Oh, I have no idea what Mr. Cuddlekins is up to. He's getting quite good with the computer. You should see how quickly he can add items—" Her luminous eyes widen, and she glances at anything in the room except me.

"Oh, please go on. I would love to hear how my

half-wild caracal is learning to control a mouse. No pun intended."

Ghost-ma pats her chest and vanishes from the visual spectrum.

"Not so fast, Myrtle Isadora. You've got some 'splaining to do!" My terrible Ricky Ricardo impression never fails to get a ghostly chuckle. Laughter echoes through the ether, but she does not reappear.

Turning to Erick, I open my mouth to see what he makes of this morning's musicality, but his phone rings and his face turns dark as he answers. "Erick Harper here — I did not. When did this occur? Understood. Has Sheriff Paulsen already been notified?"

I lift my hands and shake them urgently. I hate to be left out of juicy gossip.

My husband looks away, deadly serious. "Understood . . . And you've established a task force? Underway? 10-4. I'll reach out to Paulsen. I'm happy to help. Yeah— No— We don't want a repeat of the 1992 incident."

Two words hit my clairaudience like bullets fired from a gun. *Prison break.*

Stepping forward, I place my hand on Erick's arm and attempt to find patience I don't possess.

"Thanks for the call, Warden. We'll keep you updated . . . I agree. Thanks again." Erick ends the call and looks at me through worried eyes. The muscles in his jaw flex and he shakes his head once.

"What happened? Is it your— Alex Crenshaw? Did he escape?"

"No. He's in his cell. But three guys did escape."

"How bad is it?" I'm asking the question out of courtesy. Every fiber of my psychic body already knows it's pretty terrible.

"It's a state penitentiary, Moon. There's always going to be worse guys. But these three are bad. Responsible for two murders up in Silver Shoals, but that's only half the story."

He moves toward the settee and sits heavily as though a weight presses on his shoulders.

As hard as it is for me to be quiet, I know he needs to tell the story in his own time. Perhaps a distraction is in order?

"Could I interest you in making me some home fries and French toast?"

He looks up and nods. "I could be convinced."

Erick leads the way back to the walk-up, and I brew a second pot of coffee while he makes magic at the stove.

"These home fries are so good."

Laughter lifts the dark clouds for a moment. "You know I worked at the diner when I was in high school, right?"

My eyes widen, and then I tilt my head as I mentally thumb through a series of conversations. "Yeah, I think I did know that. So the reason they taste as good as Odell's is because you learned from the master."

"10-4."

"Speaking of high school—"

He drops his head in his hand. "Yup, everyone called me Ricky. Next question."

Letting him stew for a minute, I hop up and re-fill my coffee cup. When I return to the table, his shoulders have relaxed, and he's clearly under the illusion that the subject has changed. Oh, Ricky.

"The next question is, did you know that the girls in your homeroom had a betting pool on you?"

His gulp is audible. "What? You said you'd never use your psychic powers on me."

"Oh, no special powers were used. This was all via good, old-fashioned, small-town gossip."

Erick lifts his coffee and attempts to take a casual sip.

"My source revealed that she alone bet you'd never marry a local girl. When I mentioned I'd married you, she fired off a text alerting the betting pool of her triumphant win."

"Marcia. At the hospital." He hangs his head and mumbles. "Small towns."

"Did you marry me just to help Marcia win a

bet, Ricky?" My ability to hold a fake upset expression lasts less than a second. His dreamy blue eyes meet mine, and I collapse into a pile of snickers.

The tension in his shoulders vanishes, and he returns my volley. "I did. Marcia promised me a cut of the winnings. I should have almost $35 headed my way."

"Touché."

After I've finished my breakfast and a second cup of coffee, Erick still hasn't launched into the backstory on the escaped prisoners.

Well, it's time to begin Operation Goth Girl. "I'm headed over to the apartment to let Grams dress me like a doll gone wrong. Could you drop me off at the Emporium? In case Artemis has any idea what kind of car I drive, I thought it would be better if the Jeep wasn't in the parking lot."

Erick bites his bottom lip as he sizes me up. "Why is it I always find myself thanking my lucky stars that you and your grandmother have chosen to use your powers for good?"

"I suppose it's something to do with me being so awesome?"

"Yeah. That's definitely it. I'm happy to drop you off on my way to the office. How long will you need?"

"Well, I only need about fifteen minutes, but I'm pretty sure Grams will be hard-pressed to pull my outfit together in under thirty. So let's say forty-five minutes to be safe."

He shrugs. "What am I supposed to do in the meantime?"

"Maybe you can clean up around here. Someone left quite a mess in the kitchen." My subtle snark catches him off guard, and for a moment, his mouth falls open. Followed by laughter.

"Gotcha."

"Good one, Moon."

In the enormous closet, I find myself lying on the padded mahogany bench, staring up at the cedar-lined ceiling, wishing I had never agreed to go undercover.

You might think that picking a goth-chick outfit would be simple. Not for Myrtle Isadora.

"Grams! For the tenth time, just grab a bunch of black clothes and I'll be on my way."

One ethereal eyebrow arches sharply. "That wig will never work, young lady. Curly? Too positive. Keep looking. Somewhere in that drawer is the perfect bone-straight black wig. I swear. I know there's one in there!"

After several more minutes of searching, I find the supposedly perfect wig. I hate to admit when she's right.

"It shouldn't come as such a surprise, dear. I assembled everything in this closet."

"True. The only thing missing is a shred of privacy." Pointing to my lips, which did not move, I nod once.

She throws her hands in the air as though she's a helpless Victorian damsel in distress. "It's all jumbled up."

After three outfit tests and more bobby pins than anyone should have to manage before lunch, my outfit is complete.

As I stand in front of the full-length mirror and stare, I have to admit, I barely recognize myself.

Straight black hair with short chopped bangs. Pale white makeup on my face with black eye shadow, thick, kohl-rimmed eyes, and black lipstick. Grams even had some fabulous fake piercing jewelry. I have multiple earrings in my left ear, a wide ear cuff on my right, and what appears to be a ring through my nose.

I colored my fingernails black with a permanent marker, and I have a black T-shirt with the saying, "Today is fine, Satan." And over that, a raggedy black sweater with such a loose weave that you can just make out the words on the T-shirt. It's kind of genius.

Baggy black pants, with chains and safety pins, drag their hem on the floor over black combat boots. I have several strange silver rings on my fingers, and

I've turned my mood ring around to hide the cabochon.

Grams floats behind my left shoulder, patiently waiting for my internal monologue to end.

"Yes, Grams. What is it?"

"Magnificent. I wouldn't be able to pick you out of a lineup."

"Here I go. Let's hope this works."

Erick makes several comments about how the wardrobe brings out my inner delinquent, but I refuse to take the bait.

"Remember, hubby, you need to question Sheila Frenet — the internet threat chick."

"10-4, boss."

"Now you're talking." Leaning across the Nova, I plant a black lipstick kiss on his cheek and snicker like a cartoon character as I exit the vehicle.

CHAPTER 12

When I walk through the front door, Tadjo adjusts his scarf — today's is a flattering shade of lavender — and walks toward me with his chin held high. "Welcome to Ania's Emporium. How may I enlighten your journey?"

A brief flash of memory brings back an image of his mother uttering the same phrase. I kind of love that he kept the greeting.

"It's me. Mitzy Moon."

The inner actor immediately surfaces. Tadjo throws his arm back and opens his mouth as he utters a combination scream-gasp. "Magnificent! I'm planning a complete show around this character as we speak!"

"Not starring me. I may enjoy a little undercover work, but I'm not built for the stage."

He grins with tolerance as he fusses with my wig and giggles uncontrollably when he reads my T-shirt. "Oh, that is wicked!"

"I know, right?" Before we can continue our shtick, my phone rings. "Hey, can I take this in the back room? It's Erick."

Tadjo wags his eyebrows. "Be my guest. We have to keep that dreamboat happy."

Rolling my eyes, I disappear behind the beaded curtain. "Hey, what's up?"

"You got a minute to hear my story?" His voice is soft and close to pleading.

"Always. Tadjo's up front. What happened in Silver Shoals?"

"It was the first year you got here. Not too long before, everything went belly up with Ivy Lapointe. These guys, the escaped convicts, were cooking methamphetamine for her, but they decided they needed a side hustle."

At the mention of a side hustle, this morning's *O Brother, Where Art Thou?* soundtrack hits me, and I blurt, "Pyewacket! That song he was playing is from a movie about a prison break! He already knew!"

Erick takes the interruption in stride and gives Pyewacket his due. "How is it that cat is always a step ahead of us mere mortals?"

There's a moment of silence over the line as I'm sure we both picture Pyewacket's smug expression.

"So, what was their side hustle?"

"Yeah, right. They started breaking and entering for the purpose of committing burglary. Only high-end homes. They hit a few places in The Pines here in Pin Cherry, three or four places in Grand Falls, two or three places in Broken Rock, and then the Silver Shoals job."

The tone in his voice changes significantly when he says Silver Shoals. "You never mentioned it. Why didn't I hear about this?"

"Who knows? Maybe you were on a different case, or maybe it was when you were seeing—"

"Don't mention it." I roll my eyes and wave both hands. "What happened in Silver Shoals?"

"The gang had a very specific MO. They hit only wealthy neighborhoods. Only homes with no children. Homes where all occupants worked during the day. The gang would hit the homes mid-morning. They'd take cash, jewelry, silver, and easily transportable artwork. In and out in less than ten minutes." He takes a deep breath and lets it out slowly, as though it hurts.

I wish we were together. If I hadn't been so fired up about this undercover gig, I would've sensed his need to talk when he dropped me off. I'd give anything to place a comforting hand on his knee.

Erick continues, "The job up in Silver Shoals was wrong from the start. The husband and wife had severe strep throat. A friend had borrowed their car and promised to keep their café running that day so they wouldn't lose any money." He exhales in disbelief.

"Oh, so the car was gone, and it looked like they were at work, right?"

"Yeah. The gang broke in. They were flying through their checklists as usual, when one of them discovered the couple watching television in the primary suite." He swallows hard and falls silent for a moment. "Shot them both."

"Oh my gosh! That's terrible! How did you catch them?"

"Luckily, a neighbor had called the minute they saw the van pull up. Local deputies, led by Saul Rivera, were on scene within minutes. Unfortunately, not soon enough to save the couple."

I let the silence lie between us until he feels ready to continue.

"Somehow, they captured all three guys. One of the deputies was wounded, but survived."

"So they all went to prison for the robberies. Who committed the murder?"

"It's burglary when you enter a dwelling illegally. Not important." Erick blows air through his lips and continues, "They all touched the gun. They all fired the gun at some point during the shootout. It was like they had organized some kind of strategy before the thing even happened. They were interrogated, separately, for hours. Not one of them would crack. Never seen anything like it."

"But why did the warden call you? You're not — I don't mean this the way it sounds — but you're not sheriff anymore."

"The ringleader, Tug McAllister, has it in for me. As sheriff during this incident, I had access to case files from all the B&Es. Something didn't sit right. I remembered a strange detail from two burglaries. The ME had identified cat hair at two scenes where the owners didn't have a cat. When we re-examined the evidence, we discovered the hair belonged to an extremely rare breed of albino cat, and had been found at all but one scene. I was the one who connected all the robberies to that gang with that piece of evidence."

"Good for you! Oh, I could see why that would make an enemy of Tug. It had to add a lot of years to their sentences, right?"

"Yeah. It added over eighty years apiece."

Now I'm worried. Erick is in danger, and a gang of bloodthirsty thieves will probably stop at nothing to get their revenge. Not good. "So the warden thinks this guy might come looking for you?"

Erick takes two deep breaths. "There were a lot of officers involved in their arrest, and who testified at the trial. The warden is concerned they might have a hit list. I'm sure I'm near the top."

"What do we do? We've got to find them before they find you. We need to keep the upper hand." I can't stop myself from pacing around the Emporium's back room.

"Yeah. The warden wanted to make sure I knew what was headed our way. I'll coordinate with Paulsen and find out if she'll put me on the task force."

"Paulsen? No way. You know how vindictive she is. She'll throw the whole civilian thing in your face and leave you twisting in the wind. We need to look into this privately. We have the resources."

Despite the serious nature of this situation, my outburst draws a chuckle from him. "Don't get your heiress panties in a bundle, Moon. I know those cases inside and out. I owe it to the surviving family members to put these guys back where they belong. My check-in with Paulsen is a courtesy. If she doesn't want to play ball, she can't stop me from looking into it on my own. It's not exactly the Wild West up here, but a posse to capture escaped prisoners isn't something the public would have a problem with."

"A posse? I've never been part of a posse." Woohoo! I can't wait to tell Grams I'm gonna be in a posse.

"It's nothing to celebrate, Moon. The most important thing is putting these guys back in prison. They're extremely dangerous. We can't afford to let any more innocent civilians be placed in jeopardy."

"You're not worried about what might happen to you?"

He swallows with difficulty. "I don't think I have time to worry."

"Understood." Ending the call, I wander back into the retail area.

Tadjo picks up where we left off. "Okay. You can work behind the counter. I'll hang out in the back room in case you get into trouble. Everything is priced. My mother was obsessive. But if there's something you can't find. Let me know."

I hope Erick won't do anything rash. My thoughts are swirling wildly.

"Mitzy, everything OK?"

"Actually, no. There's something Erick and I need to handle today. I'll be back tomorrow, and we can totally set this Artemis trap. Sorry."

He fidgets with his scarf. "Don't be sorry. It

must be pretty important . . . Maybe more important than catching my mother's killer."

I recognize a pout when I see one. "It's not more important, Tadjo. It's a whole *Sophie's Choice* kinda thing. You understand, right?"

My movie reference hits home. "Meryl Streep is a celestial being. That woman can do anything. *Anything!*" He takes a breath for courage and squeezes my arm. "Go. I'll keep things going today. Maybe I could go and talk to Sheila Frenet. Would that help?"

"Absolutely not! If Sheila is the killer, I don't want you or your brother poking that bear. Leave it to Erick. He'll know what to do."

"10-4, Captain Moon."

Even though we're both stretched to the breaking point emotionally, his goofy comment gives us a moment's reprieve.

"Hang in there, Tadjo."

"And you, Mitzy."

CHAPTER 13

BEFORE WE GET TOO FAR AHEAD of ourselves in the fugitive-recovery planning, Erick insists on having a chat with Sheriff Paulsen. Oh goody! My absolute favorite.

After a quick wardrobe change and pregame planning sesh, we're ready to face the cranky, opinionated sheriff. Well, Erick is ready to face her. I'd prefer to snipe from the sidelines, but that's my inner delinquent talking.

Despite the season technically being spring, Erick takes it easy on me by piling us both into the Jeep rather than dragging me through the icy streets.

The town is fairly quiet, and there's ample parking on Main Street.

When we open the door to the sheriff's station,

we're hit with the familiar mélange of burnt coffee and dust. Furious Monkeys actually looks up from the addictive game on her phone and smiles. "Hey, what brings you two in?"

Erick steps toward the desk, and she immediately drops her phone. Apparently, it doesn't take a psychic to sense the serious nature of his visit.

He gives her the bare bones of the prison break and asks to see the sheriff.

Deputy Baird — her actual name — gestures to the crooked wooden gate separating us from the bullpen and adds, "Head on back, Detective Harper."

He nods once, holds the gate for me, and we walk solemnly toward the sheriff's office.

The station never changes. It always reminds me a touch of Sheriff Valenti's from *Roswell* with a heaping helping of Sheriff Andy Taylor's from Mayberry. Dented metal desks. Actual typewriters. Mugs of the singed brew of the day.

However, the bullpen is currently empty. The deputies must be on a call.

How many times did I force my way into this station and march back to Erick's office when he held the title? Too many times to count. There was something so right about him being responsible for the safety of this county. I can't say I feel the same about Paulsen or her motives for seeking the office.

My respectful hubby leans in and politely knocks on her open door.

She looks up, and for a moment forgets her vendetta against me.

"Hey, Harper. Have a seat." When she catches sight of me, her right hand immediately goes to the handle of her holstered gun, and frown lines crease her brow. "What do you want, Moon?"

Yeesh! If things weren't so serious, I'd give her a taste of the Mitzy Moon snark. However, today isn't about me. I want Erick to have the best chance possible of getting on this task force.

He brings her up to speed on his conversation with the warden and she nods, but my extrasensory perceptions pick up on a building resistance.

"I hear what you're saying, Harper. Problem is, you're not law enforcement. I know you've got that whole legal detective agency, but it's not the same. I can't put a civilian on the task force."

He leans in and gives off a feeling of something close to panic. It's a new sensation. I've never picked up on such a high rate of anxiety before.

"Look, Paulsen, you and I both know I'm gonna follow up on this gang regardless of what happens. It would sure look good for your office if the task force was responsible for the capture and return of these fugitives. You know as well as I do, you can make me an honorary deputy. Just until we bring these guys in. What do you say?"

Her need to be right and control the headline when the story hits the paper is stronger than her dislike of me. The metal gate in her wall of excuses is creaking open. If ever there was a time for me to keep my mouth shut, it's right now. Too bad I'm a slow learner. "Yeah, and let's not forget, I'm already an honorary deputy."

The slight opening vanishes as the proverbial steel gate slams closed. "No civilians on the task force. If you two think you have a better chance of capturing these escaped convicts than an entire team of law-enforcement professionals, I'd like to see you try."

Erick leans back in his chair and shakes his head. There's a strange shift in his energy. He rises to his full six feet and change, clenches his fists, and the voice that fills the room is gravelly and power-ful. "Protecting innocent civilians isn't about credit, Paulsen. That's one thing you never seem to un-derstand."

I'd love to take a quick pic of the shock and awe frozen on Paulsen's face, but one thing I have learned since I landed in Pin Cherry Harbor is to quit while I'm ahead. Turning on a dime, I head out of the office, and Erick is on my heels.

He waves stiffly at the recently returned

Deputy Gilbert as we pass through the bullpen. Erick is out the door ahead of me, and I offer a kind nod to Deputy Baird. She shrugs her shoulders in a way that I've come to understand means: "Sorry about Paulsen. I thought there was a chance."

Once we're back in the Jeep, the tension is thick. Time for some of my so-called humor to lighten the mood.

"That went well. Should we get started?"

Thankfully, my guy doesn't hold a grudge.

"Aaah. I thought I had her buy-in — right before my wife jumped in to help." Erick shakes his head and chuckles good-naturedly. "I should've known better. I tried to follow the proper channels and re-spect the office — no time for that now. Ready for a quick drive?"

"I was born ready, Harper."

He pulls onto Main Street as he chuckles.

I'm lost in thought. The scenery outside the window blurs, and I'm genuinely surprised when the Broken Rock city limits sign looms into view.

Erick grabs his phone and places a call on speaker.

"Harper, buddy. To what do I owe the pleasure?"

"Hey, Boomer. I'm sure you heard about the prison break."

"10-4. You on the task force?"

"No such luck."

"That Paulsen . . . What's your plan, brother?"

"Mitzy and I are going to look into things. I just need to know somebody's got my back if it comes to it."

"Always. You need me. I'm there."

"Thanks, Boomer. I'll let you know if I hear anything. You'll do the same?"

"10-4."

He ends the call and drops his phone in the cup holder.

"You think he'll really let you know what's happening?"

"Absolutely. Boomer is a good guy. But I'm worried about what happens if we find these guys. I don't think we're going to be able to bring in all three of them by ourselves. I need to know I can count on somebody — somebody who can handle a firearm."

A creepy chill races over my skin. Now that Erick has left the force, Boomer is the number one sharpshooter in the county. If Erick is already thinking that things could come to a deadly end . . . gulp.

"Wait, we're *in* Broken Rock. Why didn't you just talk to Boomer at their station?"

"We're not going to the station. I'm going to the fugitive's last known hideout."

"Hello! How about a warning before you take me into a scene from *Heat*? Maybe you need to tell Boomer to meet us there. I don't think I'm exactly ready for a shootout before lunch."

For some reason, that comment hits his funny bone, and he laughs out loud as he shakes his head. "Don't worry. If I know anything about Tug McAllister, I know he'd never return to their previous lair. I just want to poke around and see if there's anything there that might help us figure out where they're going."

"Got it. I'll help however I can."

He inhales sharply. "Wish I didn't have to drag you into this, Moon, but your special abilities might be the difference between life and death for some people out there. I'm not trying to put all this on you."

Reaching over the console, I grab his arm with two hands. "What? Nonsense. It's nothing. I'm happy to do it. I know what it means to you, and it's not like I want anyone to get hurt. We need to get these guys back where they belong as soon as possible."

Erick nods. "On second thought, I don't suppose there's any way you'd agree to sit this one out?"

"Harper! You've met me, right?"

He gives me an amused side-eye and nods. "Yeah. I met you. Fell in love with you. Married you. And despite multiple attempts, I've learned your brilliance cannot be contained."

"Touché."

Our visit to the old hidey-hole is a bust. The ramshackle cabin has long been abandoned. Nature and rodents have taken over. A search through what little remains confirms the shack once housed a cat, but otherwise proves fruitless.

Erick opens the passenger door of the Jeep for me and hangs his head in defeat.

"Hey, don't let it get you down. We eliminated one possibility. That's actually amazing. We'll find them. I promise you. Don't give up. All right?"

He nods, closes my door, and jogs around the front of the vehicle.

"What happened to the cat?"

Lost in thought, he doesn't connect the dots. "What?"

"The albino cat that helped solve the burglary cases. What happened to it after Tug got arrested?"

"Most likely animal control picked it up. Why?" He starts the engine and meanders toward home.

"Seems unfair that an innocent animal was caught in the middle of all this. Shelters aren't great, you know."

He nods absently, but suddenly his drooping shoulders square and his eyes spark with hope.

"Tug has a sister. They weren't close, but she might've grabbed the cat."

"Good thinking, Harper. Plus, that's one more lead for us and zero for the task force."

Erick smiles. "I'm glad you're on my team, Moon."

"Same, Harper. Same."

CHAPTER 14

Tucked up in my old apartment, I order delivery and update the murder wall while Erick calls in every favor he's ever been owed. While he waits for Boomer to find the contact info for the sister, he tries the county shelter.

Myrtle Isadora instantly pops into the visual spectrum. "I'm not pleased with this situation one bit. I heard everything. Definitely not pleased with the idea of you hunting down dangerous criminals! I won't stand for it!"

"Oh, is that so? Would you rather have me do nothing and take a chance that something terrible happens to Erick?"

When faced with this unpleasant scenario, Ghost-ma backpedals.

"Of course I don't want anything to happen to

Erick, sweetie! Oh, dear. Promise me you'll be careful!"

Pausing to share her concerns with Erick, I give him the opportunity to reply.

Since he can neither see nor hear my grandmother's ghost, he gazes hesitantly into the emptiness, places a hand over his phone and mouths, "We'll be as careful as we can, Isadora."

I'm eavesdropping like Samwise Gamgee on Erick's call. Sounds like animal control has no record of an albino cat being picked up in December of 2019. Erick ends the call and exhales a frustrated moan. "Nothing but dead ends."

"Hold on. Did I hear you say December 2019?"

"Yeah, why?" He's scrolling through contacts on his phone to see if he can come up with any other ideas.

"That was when you asked me to look into that hit and run. The one that paralyzed Doc Ledo." My wheels are picking up speed now.

"Is that how you remember it? Seems like you butted your way in with some questionably obtained evidence, if I remember correctly." He arches one eyebrow.

"Let's not split hairs. I'm only mentioning it because now it makes sense why you gave in so easily. You had your plate full with this burglary/murder investigation." Crossing my arms, I nod.

Erick pockets his phone and walks toward me. "Did you honestly think that the only cases we handled at the sheriff's office were the ones you worked on?" His eyes twinkle with mischief.

"No. I mean— Well— Not important. We should focus on the positive outcomes. You put Tug and his crew in jail, and I helped Doc Ledo get closure." Snaking my arms around his waist, I pull him close and hope to distract him.

"You did a good thing for the doc, Moon. You listened to what he wanted. It took some time to refurbish his clinic with adjustable exam tables and a larger surgical suite, but now he can run the entire veterinary clinic from his wheelchair." Erick kisses the top of my head.

The service bell at the side entrance heralds the arrival of our supper.

Erick returns with the food, but his expression is grim. "We can't stay here tonight. It's not safe."

In an effort to stay off the killer's radar, Erick has me calling in a favor from Twiggy.

"Hey, Twiggy. I heard you were thinking about getting another dog. Do Bartles and Jaymes need another buddy?"

"Look, kid, I appreciate your attempt at small talk, but we both know my current pet situation isn't something you're interested in. Who put the bee in your bonnet?"

"Hey, I tried. It's this whole escaped prisoner thing. Erick doesn't think we're safe at the walkup or at his old house. He doesn't want to be anywhere Tug McAllister can find us. I was wondering if we could stay out at your cabin?"

"Are you bringing that demon spawn of a cat?"

After I contain my laughter, I reply, "Nope. Mr. Cuddlekins is going to stay with Grams. They'll hold down the fort at the bookshop and let us know if Tug or one of the other convicts shows up.

"No problem, kid. You know the drill out there, and you know where I keep the key. Better pick up some firewood, though. Wayne and I haven't gotten out there to restock after winter."

"Got it. I'm sure Erick knows where to get stuff like that."

Her ready cackle rolls across the line. "Sometimes I forget what a helpless indoor kitten you are. Good thing you locked that lawman down when you had the chance."

"Ha ha. I bring a lot to the table in this relationship too."

An even more exuberant cackle is her only response.

"Well thanks, I guess."

"No problem, kid."

Ending the call, I shake my head in Erick's general direction. "I can't believe you made me do that. You must know someone with a cabin."

"Of course I do. That's the point. If it's someone I know, Tug might be able to trace it. At least there's a chance he won't figure out the connection between me and Twiggy."

"Fair point. I'll pack. When do we leave?"

He glances at his phone. "Ideally? Five minutes ago."

Taking the steps two at a time, I hustle up to the third-floor primary suite and randomly throw some of my crap in a bag. I toss the goth chick disguise in, on the off chance I can get back to the Emporium sometime tomorrow.

Nobody likes to be fleeing a dangerous criminal. But we have to get the upper hand. We need the element of surprise. So far, the map and pendulum haven't worked. I mean, I didn't even bother using them to search for Artemis. She's certainly using some kind of cloaking spell. On the other hand, Tug and his gang wouldn't know the first thing about paranormal stuff. There's still a chance I'll get a hit on the missing convicts.

Running downstairs, I toss my bag by the front door as I make my announcement. "I need to grab the map and the pendulum thing-y from the apartment. I'll meet you in the alley."

"10-4. Let's take the Jeep."

Neither Grams nor Pyewacket are anywhere to be found, so I make a general announcement to the ether. "Erick and I are headed to— Well, you know where. And you know how to get a hold of me. I love you, Grams!"

A faint voice echoes from the nothingness. "I love you too, sweetie."

Before her energy crisis, I would've ignored the change in her intensity and hit the road.

"Grams? Are you all right? You're not feeling the push or the pull from the veil or whatever, are you? You're not disappearing, right?"

She pops into the visible spectrum, clutches her pearls, and sighs. "I'm fine, dear. I happen to have a lot on my mind, and I'm having an issue with casting."

"An issue with what?"

Her glowing eyes widen. "Oh, it's nothing. You and Erick get somewhere safe. We'll have plenty of time to talk about it down the road."

Casting? Has she taken up some kind of other-worldly fishing?

As I make my way down to the side door to the alley, the hairs on the back of my neck stand on end. She's up to something. And I can already tell I'm not going to like it.

We drive to the cabin in tense silence. I sense Erick running through scenarios in his mind and thinking of ways to keep me safe. For once in my life, I let sleeping dogs lie and gaze wistfully out the window.

When we arrive at the cabin, Erick asks me to wait in the warm car while he goes through the procedure of getting the place up and running. There are valves, switches, and, of course, someone has to build a fire. I'm truly grateful for his chivalry.

Eventually, he waves me in. "Despite all the hoops to jump through to get the place running, I like it here. It's cozy. Even though it's not mine and I don't really have a history here, I somehow feel at home."

He hangs my hat and coat on one of the wooden pegs by the front door and leads me to the roaring fire in the tiny living room.

The view through the windows toward Island Lake is beautiful. This lake isn't nearly as deep as the region's great lake, and this ice has already melted fifty yards back from shore.

Some diehard angler is out in a small trolling boat, making his way between land and the receding ice. Gotta admire his commitment.

"I grabbed a few groceries from home, but I should probably run in to the Piggly Wiggly and pick up more supplies."

"Are you kidding me right now, Harper? The last thing we're going to do is separate. In every movie I've ever watched, that's when everything goes wrong. Even you know that."

He chuckles. "Fine. We'll make do with what we've got for tonight. And tomorrow—"

"Hey, is Tug his real name?"

Erick shrugs. "I'm sure it's not. Lemme think for a minute." He bites his bottom lip as his eyes dart up and to the left. "I got it. Thackeray. When I was writing up the reports, I remember thinking it was strange, and I didn't blame him for coming up with a nickname. Why?"

Gesturing wildly, I exhale. "That's why the pendulum wasn't working. I have to have the true name. Or word the question differently. Let me try again. I think it might work now. Maybe we can actually find him."

Spreading the map across Twiggy's coffee table and kneeling on the braided rug, I extract the pendulum from my backpack and wait for the chain to find its center.

As the inverted cone spins itself to stillness, I formulate the proper question in my mind. "Show me the location of the man called Thackeray McAllister, also known as Tug McAllister."

The pendulum arcs in a wide swing, eventually making large circles and pulling my hand left along the map. As we near the old Fox Mountain ski resort, the circles become tighter and tighter. Eventually, the point of the cone snaps to a place on the map as though pulled by a magnet.

"Look! He's here. He's right here!"

Erick grabs a pen from the table, marks the spot with a small circle, and pulls out his phone.

"A circle? Really? You can't even do me the favor of using an 'X' to mark the spot?"

He gives me a courtesy chuckle, but the tension in his shoulders is palpable.

"I'm gonna send this image to Boomer. I'll see if he can mobilize the task force."

"Copy that."

Sitting in silent satisfaction will have to be my sole reward. I'll take it. There was a time, not that long ago, when I couldn't even tell Erick how I got my "hunches." Now he takes me at my word, and he's so confident in my abilities that he's willing to share this intel with an official task force.

We call this progress.

CHAPTER 15

AS WE DRIVE TOWARD BROKEN ROCK, the mood ring on my left hand encircles my finger with a fiery message. Glancing down, I see the pure white fur and clear-blue eyes of an albino feline.

"I saw the cat."

Erick has both hands on the wheel, and his gaze is deadly serious as he navigates. "What are you talking about, Moon?"

His tone is tense and curt. It's not about me. I don't take it personally. It's clearly important for him to put Tug back where he belongs. Behind bars.

"The albino cat. I just saw an image of it in my mood ring."

He swallows with difficulty. "Help me out. What does that mean?"

"To be fair, it could be anything. As you know, the mood ring is hella moody. I'm going to think positive and say that it means we're on the right track. The sister has the cat and Tug is at her place."

"Come on, Moon. Boomer and his guys already checked her house. The fugitive wasn't there. None of them were there. I think — you know how much I appreciate your abilities — but I think we're on a wild-goose chase."

"Hey, I get it. I'm the one who *gets* these messages, and I still have a hard time believing in the paranormal. You have every right to be doubtful. But humor me, all right?"

Erick nods and exhales a fraction of the tension he's holding.

Before he can say yay or nay, his phone rings. "Answer it for me, will you?"

Grabbing his phone, I tap the speaker icon. "Hey Boomer, you're on speaker with me and Erick."

"I saw the text. You guys are headed back to the sister's place?"

Erick shrugs. "Not sure. I don't have her address. We're headed to a point northeast of Broken Rock. Looks like it's outside the city limits off County Road 268."

"Yeah. That definitely sounds like the place. I told you we already checked it."

Erick clenches his jaw and looks at me, so I jump in with some improv.

"Some new information came to light, Boomer."

He chuckles. "Was this new information from you, Mitzy?"

Blowing a raspberry, I rush to gather my thoughts, but Boomer beats me to the punch.

"Hey, an update came across the wire. They picked up Kurt Fagan and Cobb Hartman. The fugitives attempted to jump a train headed west. The railroad special agents grabbed them for trespassing. Just got lucky that one of them had seen the BOLO earlier today."

Erick's shoulders relax a fraction of an inch. "So Tug is the only one unaccounted for?"

"10-4. You need backup at the sister's place?"

Erick looks at me, and his eyes plead for reassurance.

I swallow hard and nod once.

He inhales sharply. "Yeah. We definitely need backup."

"You got it. Now I need a reason to head back out there . . ." Boomer hums a little tune before he continues, "I'll think of something. Oh, and I'll text you the address right now."

The call ends and the text pings on Erick's phone. When I tap the address, a pin flashes up on the map app.

Even with my sketchy orienteering skills, I can see the resemblance to the location of the circle Erick drew on my pendulum map.

As we head out of Broken Rock, we lose cell signal.

Erick glances at me and smiles briefly. "You got the address locked in that special brain of yours, right?"

"Copy that."

He uses the paper map as a reference, and when he makes the final discernible turn, he looks at me. "Now what?"

"Keep heading straight down this road. There oughta be a left-hand turn up ahead. I'll know it when I see it."

He rolls his shoulders back and exhales. "Here we go. Maybe we should wait for Boomer."

"What? Why? We figured this out. We deserve the collar."

"Hold on, Moon. Like I told Paulsen, it's not about the credit. It's about surviving. Boomer and whoever he brings with him will be armed."

Now seems like the right time to share my secret. "I happen to be packing heat if that makes you feel any better."

He pumps the brakes and stops in the middle of the deserted road. "You're what?"

Pasting on a huge smile, I attempt to make my

news as positive as possible. "My dad's been taking me to the shooting range. I already knew how to handle a gun. You've seen me shoot. I have excellent aim. And I've been keeping my skills up. I can back you up." My voice is an octave higher than normal, and my speech a rapid staccato.

Erick hangs his head and shakes it back and forth. "You're determined to die young, aren't you?"

"Rude." There's no time to tease him with my favorite line from *Knock on Any Door*, "Live fast, die young, and have a good-looking corpse." Instead, I'll have to appeal to his emotions. "I'm determined to be a good wingman. I'm determined to be backup you can count on." Tears well in my eyes. "I'm determined not to watch you die trying to uphold your standard of justice."

The tension in his shoulders melts as he leans across the console to kiss my cheek. "10-4. When we get there, you let me know what messages you're getting — where to look for Tug — but I take the lead. Understood?"

"10-4."

A tense chuckle escapes as he depresses the accelerator. "Is this the left?"

Pointing to the perfect "V" of Canadian geese veering left in the sky above us, I can barely speak through my fit of stress giggles. "Yeah. This is the end of our literal wild-goose chase."

His sense of duty is the only thing keeping Erick from joining my punchy emotional breakdown. He turns, and at the end of the road stands an old white farmhouse. The paint is peeling and faded, and a mostly collapsed barn is the only other structure on the property.

Patting my chest as I catch my breath, I declare, "He's definitely not in the barn. Too cold. Too exposed. Tug is somewhere in the house."

Erick parks a couple hundred yards from the house.

"Can you give me anything else? Anything?"

Closing my eyes, I inhale deeply and reach out with all of my extrasensory abilities.

Floating through the air like a wispy feather is one word. *Cellar.*

"Cellar. Something about a cellar. Does that make sense?"

My experienced partner glances at the farmhouse. "There are no basement windows. But this is a really old structure. It may have a root cellar. We'll see if we can talk our way into the house, then I'm not sure what to do."

I nod, and we exit the vehicle.

As Erick knocks on the storm door, the interior wooden door opens almost immediately, as though someone had been watching us approach through the window.

"Helen McAllister?"

She crosses her arms and lifts her chin. "Who wants to know?"

Erick softens his features and smiles in that way that melts hearts. "I'm sure you've been through the wringer these last few days, Helen. I know you're estranged from your brother, and I apologize in advance for asking more questions."

Her chin lowers, and about fifty percent of the suspicion in her eyes vanishes. "You're not cops?"

He shakes his head and offers an adorable chuckle. "One moment, ma'am." Erick reaches into his pocket and extracts his wallet, showing her his PI license. "My wife and I are private investigators. We're looking into things on behalf of the families. I'm sure you understand how shook up the survivors must be."

Her reaction is strange. There's a flicker of understanding, but beneath that, a roaring inferno of fear. That's all the confirmation I need. Tug is definitely here, and she's not happy about it. That's my cue.

"Helen, do you mind if we come in? It's freezing out here. We just need to ask a few questions. There might be something that you know, some name that will trigger a memory. Anything could help us."

Her defenses instantly go up, and I can see her

struggling to find a plausible excuse. Lucky for us, she comes up empty-handed. "Sure. I guess. Come on in."

She gestures to a small plaid couch. "You can sit there. I don't have coffee or anything."

Her tension is nearly off the charts. Even Erick must sense it. I attempt to calm her. "Aw, that's no problem. Don't worry about us. We'll be out of your hair in no time."

There it is, that surge of fear. That barely concealed desire to beg for help.

Erick begins with a softball. "Were you kind enough to take in Tug's cat when he went to prison?"

"I didn't have much choice. Animal control called me. Couldn't let that innocent creature be euthanized. He didn't ask to be the pet of a felon."

The tone in her voice is vehement. There's clearly no love lost between her and her convict brother.

My husband casually glances at me and tilts his head slightly toward the door. I think he's trying to get me out of the hou— No, wait! He wants me to get *her* out of the house. That means—

He lobs another question at Helen, while my brain whirrs out of control. "Helen, can you think of the last time you heard from your brother? Did he write from prison?"

She scoffs. "He sent me a birthday card. If you can believe that? He never cared about my birthday when he was out here in the real world. Didn't have time for his straight-laced sister. Once he was locked up and had nothing better to do, then he happened to notice that he'd missed about thirty-five of them."

Well, she's definitely not protecting her brother by choice. Suddenly, I catch a whiff of tobacco lingering subtly in the air.

"Helen, do you possibly have a cigarette?"

Her eyes widen. "Why?"

"I'm trying to quit, but I'm having so much trouble. I haven't had a cigarette all day and — any chance you got one?"

She smiles and nods. "I know what you mean. I'm trying to quit, too. But when I'm under stress—" Her eyes widen. The fear is palpable.

Before she says anything else, I jump in to save her. "Isn't that always the thing? Something simple, like paying the bills or having to work an extra shift. It just adds up, you know?"

She walks toward her coat. I'm assuming the cigarettes are in the pocket since there's so little odor inside the house.

Erick nods vigorously.

Hopping up from the couch, I join her. "Hey, throw on your coat and come out with me."

I sense the resistance and fear, but beneath that — there's also a tiny flicker of hope. She shoves her arms in her jacket with incredible haste, grabs her hat, and basically puts her boots on as she's walking out the door.

Looking over my shoulder, I shake my head at Erick. Hopefully, he receives my meaning. Don't take any stupid risks until Boomer gets here, is what I'm trying to say.

Once we're outside, I hook my arm through Helen's and propel her toward the Jeep. "Look, I know Tug is inside. I know he's forcing you to hide him. Deputies are on their way from Broken Rock. That guy in there, he's the former sheriff of Birch County. He can handle himself. Let's get you in this car."

She clutches my arm and bursts into tears. "Oh my God! I was so scared. When they came before — I just — He's so dangerous."

Opening the rear passenger door, I get her into the vehicle and sit next to her.

"Hey, I want you to know I have a gun. If he somehow gets by Erick, I'll do my best to protect you."

Red and blue lights flash at the end of the road. Thankfully, Boomer was smart enough to approach without sirens.

He stops at the Jeep on his way by. "How'd you get Helen out of the house?"

"Not important. Erick is in there. And Tug is in the cellar."

Helen looks at me and her jaw falls open. "How do you—?"

Patting her hand, I smile. "Just a hunch."

Boomer communicates with his team, and they take tactical positions around the house.

Before Boomer can breach the front door, it swings open and Erick emerges with his hands in the air.

Helen gasps, and it's not hard to make the leap of logic that the man pointing a gun at Erick's head is Tug McAllister.

Sinking into my extrasensory abilities, I can hear the exchange.

Tug demands that Boomer drop his weapon. Erick insists he doesn't.

Boomer drops his gun and kicks it away.

Blerg.

"Helen. I want you to get down on the floor. I'm going to try to get out of this vehicle as quietly as I can. The other officers may be entering the house and not realize what's happening. I have to help."

She offers no argument and immediately crouches.

With Helen otherwise occupied, I take a deep

breath and focus all my abilities on invisibility. It's been a while since I practiced this alchemical working, but without some *super*natural help, my natural clumsiness is sure to blow my cover.

Carefully popping the handle, I ease the door open and slip onto the ground.

As far as I can tell, Tug hasn't seen me. The invisibility thing-y is working.

"Get on your knees." Tug's voice is thick with hatred. He'll stop at nothing to keep his freedom.

When I reach the front bumper of the Jeep, I watch as Boomer lowers himself to the ground, keeping his hands in the air.

Tug still hasn't noticed me.

Erick has.

Dagnabbit! The stress has stolen my focus.

I can read Erick's face like an ad in the newspaper. He is going to sacrifice himself if it means saving Boomer.

That sequence of events is not all right with me.

As Tug moves the gun away from Erick's head and takes aim at Boomer, I step out and fire a round past Tug's shoulder.

In that split second, Erick throws his head back, smashing Tug's face as he wrestles the convict to the ground.

One second later, Boomer is on his feet. He retrieves his gun and attempts to find something to aim at as Erick and Tug wrestle for their lives in the snow.

A second gun goes off, and both men on the ground fall still.

Dropping my gun, I run forward. "Erick! Erick!"

As I reach the pile of bodies, there's movement.

Tug rolls to the side.

Erick is lying in the snow, covered in blood.

Frozen in time.

My heart stops beating. My breath is stuck in my lungs.

Boomer has one knee in Tug's back and he's slapping the cuffs on when he stops.

"That's not Erick's blood."

Boomer rolls Tug over. The escaped prisoner is bleeding profusely from a serious gut shot. The deputy immediately calls for an ambulance,

Erick lurches up, gasping for breath, and drops the gun in the snow. "He was going to take the shot. I had to do something. The gun went off as we struggled. You saw what happened, right?"

My heart sinks. "Paulsen is gonna be furious."

Boomer ignores my comment as he reaches out and grips Erick's shoulder. "You saved my life — again, buddy. You're not gonna get any complaints from me — or anybody else."

CHAPTER 16

THE DRIVE BACK to Pin Cherry is a blur. A bottle of wine and a cozy fire send me off to dreamland before I can update the rest of the gang.

When I awake from a nightmare version of the gun struggle between Tug and Erick, my strangled scream brings strong arms to my rescue.

Erick holds me and kisses the top of my head as I sob away the dark images. That was too close — even for a maverick like me.

"You're safe. We're safe." He whispers into my hair, and every fiber of my being wants to believe him.

"No. We still have to figure out if Artemis Ward is mixed up in Ania Karina's death. I have to go undercover tomorrow at Tadjo's shop. Maybe we'll never be safe." A ragged breath shakes my body.

"All we have is right now, Moon. Don't waste this moment worrying about things that are out of our control." Erick squeezes me tight as we lie back against our pillows.

"I want right now to last forever." He gently folds around me.

"Same, Moon. Same."

Big spoon. Little spoon.

Perhaps daylight will bring us a new lead.

Cut to—

As my eyes rove across Ania's Emporium, I nod in appreciation. "You really put things right. I'm surprised Paulsen let you rearrange a crime scene?"

Tadjo shrugs and casts his gaze to the ground. "Well, I may have done it before she officially declared it a crime scene. Sure, there was some tape and whatnot. But she didn't specifically tell me not to touch anything."

My dark-lidded eyes widen. "Who's wicked now?"

He grabs my arm with both of his hands and cackles almost as well as Twiggy. "You're a bad influence on me, Mrs. Moon. Now get to work."

He walks toward the beaded curtain. "Oh, my goodness! What's your name?"

As I pick up the duster tucked behind the

counter, I snarl in character, "Domino. Domino Hardee. Retail clerk."

Tadjo squeals with delight as he disappears into the back room.

My days in retail, the least of which as a broke barista, give me a shocking ability to appear busy.

"Tadjo, what time is it?"

"Exactly five minutes later than the last time you asked me, M— Domino."

"Yeah, let's keep it straight back there. There's not much point in me putting on this get-up if you're simply going to call—"

The chimes above the front door tinkle, and our first customer enters.

She makes a beeline for the counter, but refuses to make eye contact. "Um, is Ania here?"

If ever there was a loaded question. "Not today. What do you need?" It's surprisingly difficult to be as unhelpful as my character demands.

"Oh, um, will she be back tomorrow?"

"Let's say she'll be out for a while. Can I help you?" Hopefully, I have the right amount of irritation in my voice to be believable yet get some additional information.

"She was — she was making something for me."

Exhaling loudly, I turn toward the beaded curtain and call out, "Tadjo? Your mom was making something for this woman."

Tadjo emerges from the back, adjusts his periwinkle blue scarf, and smiles. "Kaye, hello! It was a tincture, right?"

A spasm of fear grips the woman in front of me, but she nods furiously.

"I think it's ready. Hold on." Tadjo disappears through the beaded curtain and returns with a cobalt blue bottle capped by an eyedropper. "Here it is. That'll be $45 plus tax. Can you ring this up, Domino?"

Without a word, I tap the keys on the register and press the card the woman hands me into the credit card slidey machine with a carbon copy receipt. You'd think, in an era of online sales, there would be a tap-and-pay or something from this century!

She signs the receipt, snatches the bottle from Tadjo's hand, and practically runs out of the store.

"What the heck was in that bottle?"

"Something we won't be offering any longer." He shakes his head and blows a raspberry.

"What do you mean?"

Tadjo gestures dramatically and rolls his eyes. "My mother was a big fan of love potions. I've always thought it was wrong to meddle in such a way. Generational differences, I suppose."

Nodding my head, I glance toward the door. I

wonder what she thinks she can accomplish by tricking someone into loving her? Weird.

A shipment of candles arrives to keep me busy. Pricing, rearranging, and sniffing take up the remainder of my morning.

By noon, my stomach takes charge. "Should I see if Angelo and Vinci's will deliver out here?"

Tadjo peaks through the beads. "Spoiler alert. They won't! Not to worry. I have at least half a pizza left over from a late-night bad decision, and Ray stopped by this morning with some pastries from Bless Choux."

"You're playing my song, buddy."

We share a laugh as we turn the sign to "Closed" and lock the front door.

Tadjo retrieves the cold pizza and pastries from the living quarters connected to the rear of the store.

"Mmm mm. What's on this pizza? I've never seen this combination on any menu in Pin Cherry."

Tadjo flutters his eyelids. "I know, right? Trust me when I tell you I've had to work overtime to bring the culture of the Big Apple this far north." He lifts a slice and channels Vanna White as he explains what we're eating. "The sauce is Alfredo with a splash of marinara. It's called a touch of rosé. Then you've got prosciutto roses, baby portabella mushrooms, sun-dried tomatoes, and roasted red peppers."

"Yum. But what about the cheese? It's not stretchy like mozzarella."

"Very good! Those would be dollops of mascarpone. Isn't it divine?"

Doing my best 1950s Hollywood starlet impression, I fan myself with one hand and press the other to my chest. "It's truly divine, darling."

Insistent knocking at our secured front door interrupts lunch, and all humor quickly drains.

"What if it's her?" Tadjo sits stiffly in his chair.

"If it's her, we keep up the ruse and see what she wants. You can handle this. This is what we practiced for. You ready, Broadway?"

The spontaneous nickname gives him a severe case of the giggles.

"Why don't you get yourself under control, Tadjo, and I'll answer the door."

He pops a salute that reminds me of my sweet Ghost-ma. "Copy that."

Now *I* have a case of the giggles.

As I approach the front door, all lingering levity vanishes. I haven't been face-to-face with Artemis Ward since—

Nope. I'm not gonna think about any of that right now. I'm Domino, the goth sales clerk. Uneager to please.

Opening the door, I step back in a huff. It's not our mark. Blerg.

EACH TIME THE CHIMES ABOVE THE DOOR TINKLE, I have to force myself not to turn. My character is a terribly UN-interested goth, not an eager-to-please heiress.

The day drags on, and my sales are miserable. A couple of crystals, a packet of incense, two bars of handmade soap, and one eagle-style feather.

Having lived in the Southwest, where New Age woo-woo trinkets are all the rage, I'm well aware that eagle feathers can only be possessed by Native Americans. So, the purveyors of paganism took it upon themselves to paint eagle feather markings on plain white feathers. If you read the fine print, it discloses the lack of authenticity, but few actually peruse the tiny disclaimer.

Tadjo peeps out of the back room and tries to talk me into wine.

"I don't really think I can condone drinking on the job."

"But I'm your boss. I insist."

"I'm happy to have a glass of wine with you at the end of the day. I have to keep my wits about me. You know, just in case."

He inhales sharply and lifts his eyebrows. "Oh, right. You're on a case."

Technically, Harper *and* Moon are on the case, but that's between me and Erick.

After dusting the entire store, twice, I'm about to call it a day when a feeling of danger knots my stomach.

I barely have time to look away before the front door opens. It's her. Every fiber of my being knows it's her.

Taking a deep breath, I attempt to put my abilities in stasis. I can't risk discovery.

The unforgettable voice calls out. "Do you work here?"

Turning with slow disinterest, I shrug my shoulders.

Artemis Ward has her auburn red hair tucked under a stocking cap. The sunglasses covering her unmistakable violet-blue eyes remain in place. "I'm looking for a book of spells."

Gesturing with as much nonchalance as I can muster, I point toward the bookshelves at the back of the store. "All our books are over there."

She frowns and wanders to the back. After scarcely a minute, she turns and risks tugging her glasses down. She peers over the rims. "It wouldn't be new. It could be a used book or something you keep in a special place."

I throw a hand toward the shelves behind me. "All of our, like, pricey stuff is in here." Taking the dust rag, I move away from the locked cabinets and poke at the statues of Isis and Quan Yin.

Behind me, Artemis clears her throat.

Turning, I give her my best side eye. "See what you want?"

She pauses and tilts her head.

I struggle to keep my breathing even and remain uninterested.

"No. Do you have anything in the back room?"

"Like, I'm not allowed back there, or whatever. I can ask the owner and have him call you. You can, like, write your number on that notepad."

Artemis tracks the direction my finger points and steps toward the counter. When she picks up the pen to write her phone number, a strange energy ripples around the room.

It takes every ounce of willpower I don't have to keep my breathing slow and ignore the nearly imperceptible display of power.

She taps the pen twice, but I continue to ignore her efforts.

As the powerful woman walks to the door, she tosses a comment over her shoulder. "I look forward to hearing from the *owner*."

The chimes tinkle behind her as she leaves, and

I swallow with difficulty. My entire mouth is dry. I have to gasp for air.

I think I played it cool. I hope I played it cool.

Approaching the tablet, I see she's written her phone number and, underneath the digits, a simple phrase. "My condolences."

CHAPTER 17

MY BRAIN HAS SEIZED UP. My heart wants to call Erick, but my head insists on calling Silas. Before I can grease the wheels, my phone rings with a call from Erick. As I tap the button, I can already sense it's not good.

"What's wrong?"

He inhales sharply. "How did you know?"

"Come on, you know the answer to that question. What's wrong?"

"I just got another call from the warden at Clearwater State Penitentiary. Alex Crenshaw is in the medical ward. He's not speaking."

"He's non-responsive? Did he get injured in some kind of fight?"

Erick grumbles. "No. Not non-responsive. He's not talking. There doesn't appear to be anything wrong with him, but he's refusing to speak. The warden said he's acting delusional. When they gave him a piece of paper, he claimed to be someone else."

"That doesn't sound good." Erick may not want a relationship with his bio dad, but this still isn't good news. "Do you think Artemis is trying to control him again — somehow?"

"No idea. I wish we knew where she was."

"Not to ruin the end of the movie, but I can tell you where she was two minutes ago. She was here! Artemis Ward came in asking for a spell book. And when she wrote her number on the notepad for a callback, she put 'my condolences' underneath. Clearly taking credit for what happened to Mrs. Nowak."

"Guess there's not much point in telling you Sheila Frenet, the lady who purchased the curse online, turned out to be a ninety-two-year-old woman on an oxygen tank." In spite of his attempt at nonchalance, I can sense his increased heart rate through the phone. "I've got to go straight to Clearwater. I'll take your Jeep since it has better traction in winter driving conditions. Can Tadjo take you home?"

"Don't you want to take me with you?"

"No. I don't know what I'm walking into. What if she is controlling him? What if he's some kind of ticking time bomb designed to go off when he catches sight of you? I won't take that risk."

"But what if he goes off when he sees you?"

"I'll be fine. You get home and lock the place down. Call Silas. Ask him if there's any alchemy to help. I don't know, just be safe. I'll do a turn and burn. That will put me home in the middle of the night. So, I'll crash at my old house so I don't scare you."

"I don't care what time you get home. Just get home. You don't have to sleep at your old place. I'll know it's you. I'll always know it's you." My heart is squeezed so tight in my chest it feels as though it can't beat.

He exhales in defeat. "Okay, I'll text you when I'm headed back. Be safe out there."

"You too, *Hill Street Blues*."

At least my quip gets a chuckle before he ends the call.

Stepping through the beaded curtain into the back room, I find Tadjo carefully organizing shelves and shelves of books. "Hey, she was here. Didn't you hear her talking?"

He turns and looks at me as though it's the first time he's seen me all day. "What? When did you get back?"

"Back? What are you talking about? I never left.

I was upfront, and Ward was here. How did you miss that?"

He turns, and the color drains from his face. "I knew I felt something. Oh, how I wish I'd listened to my mother! Obviously, this Artemis Ward cast some kind of spell that cut me off from what was happening. I thought everything was quiet, but — you could have been hurt!" He rushes toward me and grips both my shoulders. "Are you? Are you hurt?"

"I don't think so. But she basically admitted responsibility for what happened to your mother." I show Tadjo the note, and he stifles a sob as he shakes his head.

"A simply terrible woman. I hope Silas can do something about this."

"You and me both. I'll call him on the way back to my house." I smile and press my hands together in prayer pose. "So, could you give me a ride? Erick had to head out of town."

"Of course. No problem at all."

Tadjo and I quickly empty the register, put the money in the small safe in the back room, and close up the shop. We load into his BMW X3 and head back toward town.

Placing my call to Silas, I leave the phone on speaker in case Tadjo thinks of anything I'm forgetting.

"She just walked right into the store and asked for a spell book. It was so unnerving." I exhale my frustration.

"I am pleased you did not reveal yourself, Mizithra. However, I am most displeased by your actions. You have no idea how dangerous this woman could be. Using yourself as bait was a terrible choice."

"I wasn't bait. I was undercover. She didn't recognize me." I wish I didn't sound like a petulant child, but—

Silas harrumphs, and I can easily picture him smoothing his bushy mustache with a thumb and forefinger. "Not to your knowledge."

"Not the point. What do we do now? Erick is on his way to the prison to see what's happening with Alex Crenshaw. Sounds like Artemis may be trying to get her hooks into him again."

There's an irritating silence, and I look at Tadjo and shake with silent, impatient rage.

He sweetly picks up the ball for me. "Mr. Willoughby, is there anything in my mother's grimoire that will help us?"

Once again, Silas harrumphs. "I shall not remove that book from my vault until we have dealt with Artemis Ward. This entire situation could be one of her design. Its sole intent, to force our hand to remove the book from a place of protection.

There are other methods we can employ. For now, get Mitzy—"

The abrupt ending of his sentences seems odd. "Silas, are you still there?"

"Is someone following you?"

Glancing in the mirror, I see an unusual set of headlights behind us. Not unusual in configuration, unusual in that there's another car on the road at this time of day. Pin Cherry Harbor isn't a bustling metropolis, and this road into town is not heavily traveled.

"Maybe. Why?"

"I recommend you assume the worst. Do not go back to the Bell, Book & Candle."

My eyes dart to the road behind as my heart races. "You think she's following us? She—"

"It would appear your disguise was not as effective as you had assumed. Do not call again. Communicate through the quartz when you have reached safety, and from now on."

He ends the call, and the irritation in his voice still sours in my ears.

"What should we do? Can't go to my dad's place. That's literally right across the alley from mine. That wouldn't buy us anything." My brain is spinning a variety of scenarios — none great.

Tadjo lifts one finger and grins wickedly. "How about I take you out to the Final Destination?

There's nothing like a dive bar to bore someone to death!"

"Hey, that's a great idea. After an hour or two at Final D, she's bound to get bored and head off in search of easier prey."

My partner in hijinks changes his course and turns on Third Avenue, a healthy distance from my home. He takes the long way toward First Avenue, far west of my shop. After these maneuvers, it's easy to confirm we have a tail.

The parking lot of Final Destination sits nearly empty. Since the "S" in the neon sign has burned out, locals refer to it as Final De_tination. Which is probably more accurate.

We rush inside, and all heads turn. A flamboyant Broadway director and a goth chick are light years from the regular clientele.

Everyone else is in flannel shirts and deerstalkers with those cute earflaps. Mostly anglers, some dockworkers, and a handful of railroad employees. I recognize a couple of faces from the Midwest Union Railway, owned and operated by my father. However, they have no idea what they're looking at.

As I approach the bar, the towering behemoth of an owner known as Lars leans heavily on the scarred wooden surface, and it's easy to see he's about to deliver his "You'd be happier somewhere else" speech.

I'll head him off at the pass. "Hey, Daisy says to say hello." Wink.

Lars takes a closer look at me, blinks his eyes in disbelief, and offers a belly laugh of unmistakable proportions. "And what should I call you this evening?"

"Today, Domino seems to be working for me."

The barman graciously allowed me to work an undercover case as a redheaded southern belle a few years back. He nods his appreciation for my new venture. "Like I always say, Daisy's always got herself a job here as long as she needs it. Why don't you two take that pool table in the corner, and I'll keep an eye on what's following you."

Lars has decades of reading people under his large belt. He never misses a beat. His simple comment confirms that Artemis Ward has followed us into the bar.

"Thanks." Tadjo orders two light beers, which I will be forced to pretend to drink despite my dislike for the watery concoction.

Heading to the open pool table, I rack the balls and select a cue.

My impromptu date giggles. "You do that like a pro. Did you learn that from *My Cousin Vinny?*"

"False. You're thinking of *Color of Money*, where the character's name is Vincent."

He gasps and covers his mouth with one hand. "I've never met anyone who knows more about movies than me. This night is going to be divine!"

I lean down, break the balls with an eardrum-shattering clack, and knock in a solid and a stripe. "And I've never met anyone who uses the word divine as much as me. I'll take solids."

He chalks his pool cue and flashes his eyebrows. "Oh, you are fabulous."

Taking a little bow, I let the game get underway.

Erick and I have had the occasional date night at Final Destination. We both enjoy a good game of Around the World, and my years hustling pool with my stepbrother Jarrell provided me enough experience to be a legitimate threat. We often tie, but let the official record reflect that I'm at least $30 ahead — overall.

Tadjo and I continue playing pool, cracking wise, and drinking light beer. It's actually a great choice, since any legit amount of alcohol would dull my senses.

I need to have all my wits about me while under the microscope of Artemis Ward.

CHAPTER 18
ERICK

THERE'S VERY little traffic on the interstate as I head south toward Clearwater. Last time I went to visit Alex Crenshaw, I treated it as the interrogation of a prisoner. There was no emotional connection. This time, I have more information. I've looked at a man who bears a striking resemblance to me, or I guess it would be more correct to say, me to him. Whether or not he was in my life, Alex Crenshaw is my biological father.

The worst part is the buzzing little pinpricks about his guilt creeping in and causing me to second-guess the jury's verdict.

Before I met Mitzy Moon, I didn't believe in magic, alchemy, ghosts, or even psychic abilities. The idea of someone being manipulated into performing heinous acts by some outside force — complete nonsense.

Now, after everything Mitzy and I have been through, it's changed the way I think about these things. What if Alex Crenshaw was manipulated into committing murder — two murders?

My by-the-book brain can't process it. At my core, I'm a lawman. We follow the evidence. That evidence led to Alex Crenshaw.

I have to believe that's right.

What concerns me now is his refusal to speak. Could be a ploy, some trick to force me into returning to the penitentiary.

Okay. I'll keep my guard up. I'm not about to let a man who abandoned my mother when she was eight months pregnant try to manipulate me. There's no place for him in my life. He's exactly where he deserves to be.

As I continue south, signs of spring become more evident. The massive drifts of snow on either side of the highway are melting away. By the time I clock Clearwater city limits, there are patches of brown grass and low evergreen shrubs peeking through the receding snow.

The harsh lights of the penitentiary stand out starkly against the darkening sky.

Pulling into the parking lot, I grab my ID and my phone. Not sure if they'll let me take the phone in, but, since this is outside normal visiting hours, they might make an exception.

When I check in, I'm pleased to find Dominguez at the window.

She greets me with a smile and quickly apologizes for the circumstances. "I hope you get through to him. We're not sure if he fell and hit his head or what's going on. He's really confused."

"10-4. The warden mentioned that on the phone when he called. Alex Crenshaw thinks he's someone named Brian Clark? Is that another inmate?

Dominguez shakes her head and tucks a strand of dark hair behind her ear. "No. It's a guard. A guard who finished his shift the day before yesterday and is off until tomorrow."

"Hmmm. Strange." My wheels are already turning. "Have you reached out to Brian Clark?"

"I heard the warden left him a message. But Clark's big into ice fishing, you know. Most times, he heads straight out to the lake when he gets off shift. Has a nice little bunkhouse on the shore of Lake Tetonka. I'm sure we'll get it all straightened out when he comes in tomorrow."

Taking the official badge she slides through, I nod my thanks and hold up my phone. "Would it be all right if I take this in with me?"

"Yeah. I don't think the warden will mind." She

buzzes me through, and another guard walks me to the infirmary.

The warden is already inside and motions me toward one of the beds. He pulls the curtain back and gestures to the man in restraints. "Hopefully, you can get through to him, Harper."

I'm not sure how to respond, so I nod and turn away to whisper my question quietly. "Who is this man?" He seems oddly familiar. Can't quite place him . . .

The warden squints his eyes and looks at me as though I've lost my mind. "Alex Crenshaw. I was told you had visited him some months before. Don't you recognize him?"

"I'm sorry, warden. You're talking about the man in this bed right here, right?"

The warden tilts his head and takes a step backward. "Yes, Alex Crenshaw. We need to see if you can get him to talk."

Taking an unsure breath, I wish I'd brought Mitzy. I have no idea how to explain what I'm seeing. "Warden, I know how strange this is going to sound. The man in that bed is not Alex Crenshaw. Alex Crenshaw is blond, with blue eyes. The last time I saw him, his hair was cut pretty short, but he had hair. This man is practically bald, with a strip of brown hair running around the back of his head from ear to ear. He has brown eyes and a significant mustache."

The warden's face shifts from suspicion to fear. "Balding, brown mustache, and brown eyes?"

"Yeah." Pulling out my phone, I snap a picture and turn it toward the man in charge.

He gasps and steps away from me like a scared tourist encountering a street magician. "How did you do that?"

"Do what?"

"That photograph — That's Brian Clark!"

The man in the bed is nodding furiously. As the warden turns, a look of horror twists his features. "Clark? Is that you?"

The man's mouth had been moving, but no sound was coming out. As soon as the warden calls him by his name, Clark's voice returns.

"Yes! That's what I've been trying to tell everyone. It's me! It's been me the whole time. Crenshaw took my uniform, then he finished my shift before he walked right out of here!"

Now I remember. Clark was the guard who walked me back to the boardroom the last time I met with Crenshaw.

The warden grips my arm. "Wait here." He rushes out of the infirmary.

Sirens sound, and an announcement comes

over the PA for all inmates to return to their cells for lockdown.

While the warden and the guards are distracted by what suddenly appears to be another escaped prisoner, I move closer to Brian Clark, remove his restraints, and question him. "Can you please tell me everything that happened, Mr. Clark?"

"Yeah. Sure. You're the son, right? Didn't you used to be a sheriff, too?

"Alex Crenshaw and I have been estranged for my entire life. And yes, I was Sheriff of Birch County for several years. I have as much interest in recovering this escaped prisoner as you. Please tell me what happened."

"Yeah, you betcha. I'm just so glad somebody finally believes me. I mean, I was — Oh man." Clark breathes another sigh of relief, and his eyes glisten with unshed tears.

"It's over. Everyone knows you're Brian Clark. It's going to be okay. We need to recover Alex Crenshaw. Tell me what happened." He can take a minute after he tells me what I need to know.

"I met the visitor at check-in, walked her back to the boardroom. I don't know how she swung a private meeting, but somebody said she was a legal aide or something. We do that for them sometimes."

"Okay. Then what?" I know where this is heading, and I don't like any of it.

"She was pretty foxy, you know. Big red curls, eyes like violet petals, and legs—"

"Mr. Clark, spare me the poetic license. Tall, redhead, violet-blue eyes. Got it. What happened once you got into the room?"

"I asked if she wanted me to step outside. She said no. Next thing I knew, I couldn't speak. Then Crenshaw's cuffs fell off like they were made out of tissue paper, and she walked over — smiling — and placed her hand on my forehead. That's the last thing I remember. When I came to, I was in Crenshaw's prison uniform, cuffed to the table. The hot chick and Crenshaw were gone. I tried to scream for help, but I couldn't make any sound."

"How did you get out of the room?"

"Eventually, Parzych came to check on me. He yelled at Carlson for leaving Crenshaw in the boardroom, and they took me to his cell. I was fightin' like mad. Trying to explain who I was. But they didn't recognize me, and I couldn't speak. It was scary. Felt like I'd lost my mind."

"I'm sorry that happened, Mr. Clark. That must've been extremely stressful. Were you able to convince the guards who you were?"

"Nope. I kept making a sign for a pen and paper, but they just locked me up. So this morning, I didn't get up for morning exercises or breakfast.

They came in and roughed me up, but I still couldn't speak."

"Were you hurt?" I'd hate to think Crenshaw's escape plan actually injured this man.

"Nah. I'm tough. But when I still wasn't talking, they thought something was really wrong with me and brought me to the infirmary. The doc finally gave me a piece of paper, and I wrote down what I'm telling you. But they all laughed and said stuff like, 'How stupid do you think we are, Crenshaw?' You know, stuff like that. They didn't believe me for a minute."

His story makes sense. I'm sure the guards have to deal with all kinds of antics. "And why do you think they called me?"

"I told them to. Well, I wrote it down. I told them that Crenshaw had escaped, and if they didn't believe me, get Erick Harper down here. I had no idea what would happen. I was just trying anything, you know?"

"I'm glad you thought of it. It was smart. When you're finished with your term here at the prison, you should reach out to Sheriff Paulsen. She could use a guy like you on the force up in Birch County."

"Thanks. I haven't given much thought to what I'll do when I finish here. A lot of guys just keep going, you know? Do their time and get a pension."

"Hey, I'm not telling you how to live your life, Clark. Just saying your brain might be wasted here."

It lifted a bit of the guilt over my father's actions when I saw Mr. Clark smile.

"You think they'll catch him?"

"They won't be the only ones looking for him. And I'm undefeated in the capturing escaped convicts game."

"I'm sure glad you showed up when you did. If there's anything I can do, Harper, you let me know. I'll never be able to repay you for what happened here today. You literally saved my life."

As I walk back to the Jeep and drive northward, my mind races through all the potential dangers facing Mitzy Moon. She has enough trouble keeping safe when there's no one out to get her. But now that I know there are at least two people on her trail . . . She's likely in ten times as much danger.

Can't hurt if I break a speed limit or two getting home.

Grabbing my phone, I make a quick call to Mitzy to let her know I'm on my way.

Straight to voicemail? Huh. Guess I'll leave a message.

"Hey, I'm heading home. I'll fill you in on the details when I get there, but it looks like Alex—

"Oh sh**!"

CHAPTER 19

GLANCING TOWARD THE CORNER OF THE BAR, I'm disappointed to see Artemis Ward hasn't given up the hunt.

"Tadjo. I'm gonna get you another drink."

"I still have half a beer left, honey." He tilts his bottle toward me.

"I have a plan, and I need to make sure Lars is in the loop."

Tadjo grins, clearly excited by the promise of adventure. "I'll rack the balls." He giggles at the word, as I make my way to the bar.

Lars opens two more beers while I fill him in on my plan.

Making my way back to the pool tables, I place a quick call to my father. "Dad? Can you do me a favor?"

He says he'll never run out of favors for me. I really love him.

"Cool. There are a couple of guys from your rail yard here. Pretty sure the one with the tattooed head is Anthony Jenkins. I need them to start a bar-room brawl."

It doesn't take a psychic to predict my father's protest. After all, his entire foundation is built on getting ex-cons second chances. He certainly wouldn't put them in legal danger.

"I know. I don't want Anthony to get into trouble, either. But Lars promises he won't call the cops. I told him I'd cover any damages. Thing is, I'm in trouble, Dad. I can't get into the details. But I need a big distraction so I can sneak out the back."

At the mere mention of my jeopardy, my father's all in. He promises to text Jenkins and set the wheels in motion.

When I return to the table, I hand Tadjo his light beer and lean close as he grabs the bottle. "Be ready to run."

His eyes widen, and he attempts to tug the bottle from my hand.

I whisper one more instruction before I let go of the beer. "Seriously, play it cool. I'll grab your hand when it's time to go."

He shimmies his shoulders and winks. "I am as ready as ever!"

We continue our game of pool, when suddenly a shouting match breaks out on the other side of the bar. Jenkins slides out of his booth and pokes his thick finger into the unforgiving chest of one of the longshoremen.

A shoving match ensues, and Anthony hauls off and lands a roundhouse.

The longshoreman stumbles back.

A couple of his buddies catch him.

Within seconds, the entire bar erupts. Even local anglers get in on the commotion.

When I reach for Tadjo, he's attempting to join in the brouhaha. His arm is poised above his head, and he's about to smash his beer bottle on an unsuspecting fisherman's head.

Grabbing Tadjo's hand, I pull him away from certain death and we run through the commotion toward the story-scarred wooden bar.

Lars shoves us straight at the rear entrance and steps in front of the hallway to prevent anyone from following us.

When we burst through the back door, Tadjo is flushed with excitement.

"Did you see me? I was about to smash my—"

Pulling him toward the BMW, I scold him. "Yeah, I saw. We weren't supposed to get involved in the shenanigans. The brawl was the distraction."

He laughs until tears leak from his eyes and

taps the button on his key fob that starts the engine. "This is as close to owning Michael Knight's KITT car as I'll ever come!"

We jump in, and he floors it out of the parking lot.

Unfortunately, all of the BMW safety features prevent a movie-worthy fishtail.

"Where to, fellow fugitive?" He looks across the car at me, still buzzing from our escape.

"You can drop me off in the alley by my bookshop. I'll probably stay at my dad's until Erick gets home. Thanks again for hanging out with me tonight."

Tadjo grips the steering wheel with both hands, leans back, and sighs. "Any time. Honestly, that was the most fun I've had since I left New York. The rumors about you are true, you know."

Gulp. "And what rumors would those be?"

"Haven't you heard? More than one person has mentioned to me that Mitzy Moon is the perfect wildcard for Pin Cherry Harbor."

"Well, it's not terrible. I'll take it."

He stops in the alley, and I hurry to the metal door leading to the Duncan Restorative Justice Foundation.

I'm still fumbling with my key when the door opens. My father grabs my arm and pulls me inside before I have a chance to wave goodbye. I can hear Tadjo backing out of the alley.

"You said you were in trouble. What kind?"

"You know what I love about you, Dad?"

He slips an arm around my shoulders and leads me into the marble-lined elevator lobby. "No, but I'd love to hear it."

The elevator takes us toward the penthouse. "I love that you help first and ask questions later."

The doors ping open, and as we step into his lavish suite, he grabs my hand and turns toward me. "I guess it's a good thing and a bad thing. It's pretty much exactly what got me into trouble with Darrin MacIntyre."

That's a not-so-subtle reference to the big box store robbery he took part in. The one that landed him in Clearwater State— "Oh my gosh! I haven't heard from Erick."

Without a second thought for what my father had been saying, I yank my phone out of the pocket of my coat and instantly see the missed message. "Shoot! I missed a call from him. And there's no follow-up text."

Putting the voicemail on speaker, my father and I listen together and exchange looks of horror when Erick shouts an expletive, and everything goes silent.

"What happened? Do you think he's injured?"

Jacob rubs both of my shoulders, and his grey eyes look deep into mine. "You need to stay calm, sweetie. Take a deep breath and see if you can use your abilities to figure out what happened."

My heart is racing, and I feel like tears are about to burst from my eyes at any moment. Remaining calm sounds about as realistic as time travel.

However, my father's steadying hands on my shoulders and his own deep, calm breathing help me find my center. After another minute of panic, I can start to control my breathing. After another minute or two, a calm washes over me.

"All right, I got it under control. Thanks, Dad."

Jacob takes a step back and gives me room to get in touch with my abilities.

Slipping into a psychic replay of Erick's voice-mail, I tune into the sound of his voice and hold my focus as the call ends.

"A deer! He was in a car accident. He could be unconscious!"

My father instantly pulls out his phone. "Warden, Jacob Duncan. I believe Erick Harper was there visiting— What? Escaped? How? . . . Got it. Unfortunately, that's not the end of the bad news. It seems like Mr. Harper hit a deer on his way out of town. Can you get the local deputies up there to make sure he's all right?"

My father looks at me and gives a thumbs up.

"Thanks, Warden. Looks like I'll owe you another one."

The fact that my father, an ex-con who served fifteen years in that prison, would immediately call the warden and call in a favor — for me — these are all the reasons I'm glad I let him back into my life. Sure, I grew up eventually believing my father had died. My mother never talked about him. But it wasn't malicious. She simply had confidence in herself and her ability to raise me. She never could've predicted her untimely death. When I ended up in Pin Cherry Harbor, Silas introduced me to my living father. It took me a minute to be all right with all of it. But now, I wouldn't trade this for the world.

My father's large hand slowly waves in front of my face. "Hey, are you in there, sweetie?"

"Sorry. Just thinking about how lucky I am to have you in my life. Wait, someone escaped from the penitentiary? Are these the robb— I mean, burglary gang guys?" The phone call I just overheard is suddenly rushing back to me like a huge wave crashing against the shore.

"Didn't sound like a gang. This was just one guy. That's what Erick discovered. A legal aide came to visit Alex Crenshaw a couple of days ago. Somehow, the guard who was responsible for putting Crenshaw back in his cell after that visit didn't do his job. They found him in the locked boardroom later and he couldn't speak. That's why Erick went down there."

"Yeah, I knew that much. But Crenshaw escaped before Erick got there?"

"Yup. The warden said that when Erick got there, he identified the man they all thought was Crenshaw as Brian Clark. A prison guard."

"That means—"

"Yeah, I suspect some kind of supernatural trickery. You better call Silas."

After quickly bringing my father up to speed on Artemis Ward, the attack on Mrs. Nowak, and everything Silas is doing to protect me, I explain my dilemma. "So, I'm not supposed to call him. But I can't explain all of this through a crystal, right?"

"Call him." Jacob's confidence convinces me.

My father motions for me to put the call on speaker.

Harrumph. "It's the middle of the night, Mizithra. Not to mention the minute detail of my instructing you not to telephone."

Jacob replies. "Hey, Silas, Mitzy's dad here. She's got someone following her. Sounds like that Artemis Ward person. And we just got word that Alex Crenshaw escaped from the penitentiary two days ago. Oh, and Erick was in a car accident on his way back from Clearwater. We're waiting for details."

There's a heavy silence, and I can almost feel my mentor's power swelling through the phone. "This is most unfortunate. Artemis Ward, on her own, was enough to battle. If she has threaded her tendrils into Alex Crenshaw once again, she can effectively be in two places at once. Please keep Mizithra safe. Let me know as soon as you hear any news regarding Mr. Harper."

My heart sinks. "Thanks, Silas. We will."

After I end the call, my father heads to the refrigerator. "Can I get you a late-night snack?"

"I'm all right. Thanks though. I think I'm gonna run across the alley and change. This wig is itching like the dickens, and all of this black eyeliner is kind of starting to gunk up in the corners of my eyes. Let me get into my regular wardrobe and I'll come back for a sleepover. Sound good?"

He grins and crosses his arms. "Boy, sure would be handy to have one of those Frida Kahlo/Diego Rivera walkways right about now, wouldn't it?"

I can't help but laugh. My father's been pushing for some sort of skywalk to connect our buildings on the third floor ever since he moved next door. Don't get me wrong. I love having him across the alley, but I'm not quite ready for him to have direct access to my walk-up.

"Yeah, that'd be swell. Let's keep it on the back burner for now." Walking to the elevator, I press the call button and turn. "Back in fifteen minutes. You can time me if you want."

The thought of how quickly Erick would've whipped out his phone and taken my challenge squeezes my heart with pain for a moment, but I keep it together.

"You got it. I'll work on some hot chocolate and maybe heat up a frozen pizza?" My dad tilts his head like an eager puppy.

"Copy that."

The elevator zips me down to the first floor, and I hurry past the life-size statue of my grandpa, Cal Duncan. When I open the alley door and step out, the air seems too still.

The moment I realize why, it's too late.

A swirling glow surrounds me, while surprisingly strong hands shove me into the back seat of a vehicle.

If I could move, I'd leap right back out as the driver races around, but I can neither shout for help, nor move my limbs.

The driver's door opens, and, as I fully expected, Artemis Ward takes the wheel.

CHAPTER 20

Looks like I'll never live this down! Safety was within my grasp, but I chose to risk it all in search of more comfortable clothes. Maybe that's what they'll put on my tombstone.

A breathy chuckle from the front seat grabs my attention and annoys me.

"Don't worry, you're far more useful to me alive than dead. I'm dealing with an unusually wise old bird. I'm quite certain Willoughby won't strike to save a dead worm."

The instant she responds to my unspoken thought, I breathe deeply and empty my mind. If I do nothing else before I die, I will keep my mind blank and refuse to help lure anyone else into her trap.

Artemis taps the brakes and glances at me from

the corner of her eye. "Interesting. One would hardly train a useless heiress to hold her mind blank. Perhaps you are more than a source of funding to Silas Willoughby." She turns and presses the accelerator. "I'm thrilled with how much help you've proven to be."

Blerg. Blank. Blank. Blank.

My efforts are stellar for well over fifteen minutes. However, when she turns off the main road onto a barely plowed, unmarked side road, the bumping and jostling breaks my concentration.

I wonder if anyone's heard from Erick? What happened? Did he hit the deer or swerve to avoid it? And if he swerved, did he hit something else?

My captor tilts the rearview mirror to get a better look at me. "Are you saying something might have happened to Crenshaw's spawn?"

Blank. Blank. Blank.

"You're only hurting yourself by withholding information. Although, it doesn't much matter to me what happens to the little whelp. As long as Crenshaw thinks I'm sparing the child, I can continue to use the rod to manipulate him."

Two can— What is her beef with Pin Cherry Harbor?

"A telepathic interrogation. Wonderful!" She shimmies her shoulders and inhales deeply. "This is the perfect road-trip story, *Domino*." Artemis hums with glee.

Blank. Blank. Blank.

"I grew up believing my mother was my actual mother. At the tender age of eight, I began to question the situation. The woman changed her story to adoption. This pacified me for several more years. At thirteen, I began to experience visions, telekinesis, and mind reading. It was that last one that finally unveiled my 'mother's' true identity."

Despite my situation, my heart goes out to the child she once was.

"Compassion is poison. The sooner you learn that, the safer you'll be." Her voice cuts like a knife.

Blank. Blank. Blank.

"Anyway, I uncovered the truth before my fourteenth birthday. The woman who raised me had been an obstetrician. She'd miscarried three times, despite doing everything right. One day, she snapped. The day I was born — to be precise."

How awful! Blank. Blank. Blank.

"Awful? It was vile. She took me. Stole me from the hospital and ran. Created a whole new life working in retail under a new identity — thousands of miles from my actual family. She stole my life! I had to find my real mother. Somewhere inside me, I knew I came from magic. I wasn't about to let some muggle steal my power."

All right, clearly a Harry Potter fan. But why come to Pin Cherry?

"Oh, the last thing I pried from my kidnapper's memory was a flash of the Pin Cherry Harbor Hospital sign." Artemis grins with satisfaction.

Maybe— Blank. Blank. Blank.

"On my fifteenth birthday, I lit the house on fire, hopped a bus out of town, and never looked back."

I can only think of one other time I've been so close to pure evil. Oops. Blank. Blank.

"There have been others? Do tell. I love juicy gossip. Clearly, my predecessor was unsuccessful. The wizard Silas Willoughby still lives."

The car bumps to a halt, and, through the coils of energy entrapping me, a humble log cabin with boarded-up windows is visible. If I had to go with my first guess, I'd say it's not a cabin owned by Artemis Ward. But she doesn't strike me as the type of woman who bothers with silly little things like ownership.

"And you would be absolutely correct. I learned a long time ago that possession is nine-tenths of the law. And I possess what I wish, when I wish."

At the mention of taking what she wants, my thoughts turn to the lyrical, magical tailor Rivail and the quiet, cat-loving Penny, who both lost their lives the last time Artemis visited.

"So you were acquainted with the tailor and the witch?" She hums with a sickening pleasure. "The Bishop and the Rook. Easily captured, and their paltry powers absorbed by the victor."

She chuckles. I groan.

"It was terribly disappointing to discover the Knight had passed on before I could ferret him out. Who knows what I could've learned from that research-laden brain? I was thrown off course for a while, but everything kept pointing back to Pin Cherry Harbor. And once I delved deeply into what I had taken from the Bishop and the Rook, one name threaded them together. Silas Willoughby."

Blank. Blank. Blank.

"Empty your mind all you want, Miss Moon. Once I uncover the incantation that awakens the Eye of the Priestess, I will see Silas Willoughby and his cloaked whereabouts quite clearly. Your help will no longer be required. The knowledge I'll acquire from the Queen will lead me to my all-powerful mother. Silas can't escape me. The incantation reveals all."

Why did I take that picture?

I can't move. I can't do anything. And I stupidly thought about—

The passenger door opens, and Artemis yanks me from the back seat. She quickly frisks me and discovers my phone. Whatever power she possesses requires no fingerprint or facial recognition. Within seconds, she's into my photos.

"Would you look at that! You're phenomenally incompetent. Clearly, you *are* only an assistant. You had me going for a moment there with that blank mind trick. But only an absolute imbecile would take a picture of the very incantation I seek."

Tears well in my eyes, and I can't believe how quickly I brought down the careful house of cards.

"No use crying over spilt milk, dear. Let me get you inside and tied to a nice wooden chair. I'll need to focus all my energy on casting this spell."

Blank.

"Suit yourself."

With her hand propelling me, I march like a wind-up toy soldier, and as soon as she's secured my wrists and ankles to a sturdy oak kitchen chair, she releases the swirls of magic that hold me.

I test my bonds, but they are painfully snug.

Artemis Ward retrieves a small trunk from her car. From its interior, she extracts a cauldron not much larger than a coffee mug, a ceremonial athamé, a bundle of sage, and several small vials.

Keeping my mind as blank as I can, I wait for the key item.

As she extracts the Eye of the Priestess from a purple velvet bag, she glances toward me and shows it off like a grandparent with a photo of their favorite grandchild.

"Isn't it divine? I mean, truly magnificent! Crafted by the hands of the goddess Isis herself." She holds the orb in her palm and then presses it to her chest. "I think I'm in love."

Gag.

She purifies her space, herself, and her instruments with thick puffs of sage smoke, casts a protective circle, and then sets about studying the incantation on my phone.

The minutes are ticking away, and I may only have one chance. Closing my eyes, I send an urgent plea to my furry overlord. *Pyewacket, if you can hear me. It's too late. She has the Eye and the incantation. Tell Silas to save himself.*

"This Pyewacket, is he another one of Mr. Willoughby's assistants?"

Blank. Blank. Blank.

"What have you done?" She storms toward me, breaking the sanctity of her precious circle. Energy crackles around her as the sacred space crumbles.

She pauses, tilts her head, and the corner of her lip curves up in a snarling grin. "There is no Pyewacket. You foolish girl. All you've done is set me back a couple of minutes."

Artemis returns to her trunk and pulls out a thick scarf.

I already know where it's going, and I struggle against my restraints.

"I can't have you causing any more trouble. Let this gag be a reminder that your words and thoughts are unwelcome here." She tugs the scarf tight against my mouth and ties it in a double knot at the base of my skull.

Returning to her incantation, she begins the purification process anew. Artemis casts her circle and begins adding pinches and drips of various components to the tiny cauldron at the center of her sacred space.

Blank. Blank. Blank.

She glances at me and grins with satisfaction. She clearly prefers a docile captive.

CHAPTER 21
ERICK

"Hey, Mifflin, looks like our guy's coming around. Let's see if he knows his own name."

I hear an unfamiliar voice. It sounds so far away. The words seem as though they're coming from a distant room. And there's light . . .

"His respiration is 26 breaths per minute, down from 35. His heart rate is 113 bpm, down from 128. He's coming out of shock."

Shock. Who's in shock? Are they talking about me?

The images above me slowly come into focus, and all my years in law enforcement quickly confirm I'm in the back of an ambulance. Not as a passenger. I'm the patient. Two IV bags dangle above me, and I feel intermittent pressure on my left arm, which must be a blood-pressure cuff.

A quick internal risk assessment identifies a sharp and throbbing pain in my head. I don't feel anything else of concern, although that could simply mean I don't have feeling.

The emergency medical tech beside me leans in. "Hey, buddy. You were in a car accident. You cracked your head pretty good on the steering wheel. Looks like you'll need stitches. We put a little butterfly tape on there for now. Can you tell me your name?"

"Erick Harper. Sergeant. 491—"

"Easy, buddy. I served, too. You're in non-enemy territory. Just an ambulance on your way to the hospital. No need for the name, rank, serial number song and dance. Like I said, you have a head wound that they'll want to check out. Definitely a concussion, but everything else looks okay. They'll do an x-ray to make sure you didn't break a rib or anything. You're safe."

Taking a deep breath, I let that word sink in. Safe. Safe and not in enemy territory. Okay. I can deal with this. "What about the deer?"

The paramedic scrapes a loose brown hair behind her ear and chuckles. "Did you hear that, Mifflin? He's worried about the deer."

The driver of the ambulance laughs, and the woman pats my shoulder. "We'll have to take your word for it on the deer. When we arrived on scene, we found your car buried in the snow and wrapped neatly around a call box that should've been removed last year. There was no deer and no second vehicle."

Another wave of relief washes over me. "My head really hurts."

She checks the IV, and I wonder if they're giving me something for pain along with the saline, but I don't ask.

The paramedic checks my vitals before responding. "Seems like you're coming out of the initial shock, Mr. Harper. You must be one of those calm-under-pressure guys, right?"

"Army. Afghanistan. Two tours."

The knowing look in her eyes and the slow nod say everything. "Same part of the world. One tour for me. Is there anyone we need to call?"

Thoughts of Mitzy worried sick at home send my heart racing.

"Hey, Harper, I need you to keep taking deep breaths and stay calm. You were alone in the vehicle. No one else was injured. You didn't hit the deer."

"Did you get my phone?"

She smiles. "Yeah, it wasn't easy to find. Wedged between the crumpled dash and the smashed windshield. But these days I take it for granted that people have a phone with them. I always search a little harder, if I can. I know it can be a comfort to be able to reach your loved ones."

"Thanks. I didn't catch your name?"

"Call me Dunder."

I offer a weak grin.

Dunder reaches into a small bag attached to the side of the gurney. As she removes the phone from the bag, her eyes widen. "You seem to be getting a video call from a — cat. Should I answer?"

My head hurts too much to think up a cover story. "Yeah. Let's see what that's about."

She answers the call and turns the phone toward me.

In the center of the screen, are the large golden eyes of Pyewacket. And even without my wife's psychic abilities, I can tell he's in distress.

"Hey, buddy, something wrong?"

"Reow." Can confirm.

"Okay. There's not much I can do right now. Got myself in a bit of an accident. Don't tell Mitzy, but—"

"REE-ow!"

I'm nowhere near as able to understand him as my wife. The mere mention of Mitzy's name caused his agitation level to triple. There was an edge of retribution to the tone. Not good. With my biological father escaping from prison, his former magician's assistant turned deadly sorceress on the loose, and now Pyewacket acting vengeful—

"They're taking me to the hospital, Pye. I'll try to call Mitzy, and—"

"R-oooow."

"That doesn't sound good . . . Maybe I should call Silas?"

"RE-OW!" Game on!

"Sounds like you already did that." Maybe it's the head injury, but it feels like I'm getting the hang of caracal speak.

"Reow." Can confirm.

The paramedic holding my phone peeks around the screen and tilts her head. "Hey, I'm starting to think that you might have some lingering side effects from that head injury. This conversation you're having with a cat . . . Why don't you hang up now, and I'll run another concussion protocol on you."

"I gotta go, Pye."

She ends the call and slips my phone back into the small bag. With an understandably concerned look on her face, she runs through the concussion protocol.

I've done this so many times on suspects and victims, including running it on my wife one time — before we were married. I feel like I'm doing pretty good, but I suppose that's what everyone with a head injury thinks. "You definitely have a concussion, Harper. I'll leave it up to the doc to figure out how severe it is."

"Thanks, Dunder. What about my car?"

"They'll tow your car to the impound lot in Clearwater. Because you were involved in a no-fault vehicular accident, you'll have an additional seventy-two hours to retrieve it without penalty."

"Yeah, I know the drill. Used to be the sheriff up in Birch County."

"Oh, yeah? You're that Harper. Now I recognize the name. What are you doing now? Besides talking to cats and avoiding imaginary deer in the middle of the night."

As I attempt to chuckle along with her, a sharp pain in my head brings a rapid end to my efforts. "It's a long story. Involves a woman."

She arches an eyebrow and smiles. "Would this be a woman of ill repute?"

The phrase and an image of my wife cause laughter despite the pain in my brain bucket. "Not like you think. She's got a heart as big as the Mississippi, but she tends to leap before she looks. I resigned as sheriff. We ended up opening a private investigations agency together."

"Good for you. I bet you and your wife are doing great things up there. Will she be able to pick you up when they release you from the hospital tomorrow?"

I struggle to sit up, but Dunder places a firm hand on my chest and pushes me back to the gurney. With a heavy sigh, I hope for leniency. "I'm going to need them to release me sooner than tomorrow."

"You'll have to pull some real strings to get that done. Anybody who's had a head injury, like the one you suffered, wouldn't be cleared for driving."

"10-4. Guess I'll call my father-in-law."

Once again, the paramedic pulls my phone from the small bag. This time, she hands it to me. After negotiating the tubes and wires involved in checking my vitals and giving me fluids, I finally get the phone into a comfortable position and place a call to Jacob Duncan.

"Hey, Jacob— Whoa! Whoa. Slow down. No . . . Well, I was on my way back— Disappeared?" Figures. The minute I leave town, Mitzy gets herself in over her head. I need to get back to Pin Cherry ASAP! "They won't clear me to drive— Oh, sorry. I skipped a step. I swerved to avoid a deer on the interstate and wrapped Mitzy's jeep around a defunct call box. Yeah, I agree. That's the least of our worries right now. Can you come and pick me up at the hospital in Clearwater?"

Covering the phone, I glance at Dunder and

mouth, "Clearwater General, right?"

She nods once to confirm.

"Clark? The prison guard? Yeah, I guess he does owe me. That would be a heckuva lot quicker. You got his number? The warden? 10-4. I'll be ready to go the minute he arrives. Thanks."

Dunder reaches for the phone, but I hold it tight. "I gotta hang onto this. There's a situation developing back home. Can't afford to miss a call."

She glances at the machines monitoring my vitals. "Okay, but I need you to take some deep breaths, Harper. Your respiration and heart rates are spiking. If you can't get yourself squared away, I'll have to increase the pain meds."

"Don't do that. In fact, shut them down. I need my wits about me."

She clamps off one of the IV lines as I focus on a tiny image of my favorite childhood pet. I had a potbelly pig named Casserole. He was the smartest, sweetest animal I've ever known. He had an unfortunately brief life, but he was the epitome of calm. Whenever I find myself getting flustered. I just picture his sweet face and everything seems to settle.

"You're doing great, Harper. Keep it up."

The ambulance comes to a halt.

"We're going to unload you. You got a good hold on that phone?"

"Yeah, like someone's life depends on it."

CHAPTER 22

IF SILAS WILLOUGHBY were here now, he'd know exactly what to do. My interpretation of the unfolding events is a bit more muddled. It appears Artemis Ward has focused her entire being on the decoding of the complicated spell.

There is an upside. I know; it took me a while to find it too.

She's distracted. She's no longer pulling the Ghost-ma thought drop.

My mentor taught me how to remove handcuffs using a simple alchemical transmutation. It's time to see if a variation on that theme will work with rope.

Closing my eyes and taking two deep breaths, I focus on the ropes holding my wrists and ankles tightly to the sturdy wooden chair.

The first idea that comes to me is a cucumber

tendril. I remember reading about it in a botany book that belonged to foster father number eight. The tendrils start out straight, and creep across the ground in search of something solid to wrap themselves around. In this way, they give the plant a strong anchor and let it continue to creep toward sunlight.

I need to be something non-solid. I need to trick the rope into releasing my vaporous wrists and ankles and continuing their search.

As soon as I complete the "cucumber vine" movie in my mind, the ropes fall to the ground.

Not a moment to lose!

Lunging toward the small table, my hand pierces through the sacred circle, and it feels as though I've shoved my arm into electrified Jell-O. Pushing with all my might, I grab my phone and sweep my arm across the table.

The altar and all it held lie in ruins.

Artemis screams with the haunting wail of a banshee.

I learned one thing from all my years of watching movies and television programs . . .

Never. Look. Back.

I'm out the door! Ripping the scarf from my face, I race toward her car as I shove my recovered phone into my coat pocket.

Doors are unlocked!

With my left hand, I reach up to the visor and, with my right, to the ignition. Bingo! Yahtzee! Keys are in the ignition.

Twist. Vroom.

I slam the transmission into drive and floor it. The sedan fishtails, but I use my father's counter-steering technique to get the vehicle under control on the snowy drive.

Screams and crackles of electricity erupt behind me. Once again, I don't look back.

However, I risk a quick glance in the rearview mirror as I'm gunning it away from the cabin.

Artemis Ward is encircled in blue forks of lightning. My only hope is distance.

Attempting to press the accelerator pedal *through* the floor, I hit the pavement of the main road, swerve dangerously, and nearly lose control — but don't.

Mama, if that was you keeping those wheels on the road . . . Thank you!

Accessing my foggy memory of the ride out, I head back toward what I hope is Pin Cherry Harbor.

Once I've put a few miles between the psychotic sorceress and me, I risk a call.

It probably should've been to Silas. That would've been what was best for the world, but what is best for my heart is to call Erick Harper.

He answers in the first nano-second of the first ring. "Mitzy? Where are you?"

My lungs suck in air, but my coping mechanism is snark. "Nope. That's not how we're going to play this, Harper. You tell me why I had a vision of you hitting a deer, and why you— You first."

His relief-filled chuckle is all I need to hear. "I'm good. They're taking me into surgery."

"What!?"

"Settle down, Moon. Just a cut on my forehead. I'm a little vain, so I asked for a surgeon to close the wound rather than the ER nurse."

"Ricky Harper! I had no idea you were so concerned about your looks." The banter is helping to calm my nerves.

"Hey, just trying to protect your investment."

"Touché."

"Anyway, I'm in the medical center in Clearwater. Brian Clark is going to drive me home. They won't clear me since I have a concussion."

"Brian Clark?" He was out making friends while a magic-crazed woman held me hostage?

"Hey, it's a long story. I'll fill you in when I see you. Which will be absolutely as soon as humanly possible.

"Copy that. I'll see you when I see you."

"Whoa, not so fast, Moon. What's going on with you? Your dad said you disappeared."

"I didn't disappear. Technically, I was kidnapped. But to-may-to, to-mah-to."

A hint of tension returns to his voice, but he still chuckles. "I should've known."

"Yeah, Artemis Ward is not to be trifled with. She has the Eye of the Priestess, and, for a hot minute, she had the incantation, which I stupidly took a picture of with my phone."

"Hey, hey, don't beat yourself up. We all made mistakes tonight. I was driving too fast and trying to make a phone call, when I should've been paying attention to the road. You're safe now, right?"

"I am. Just trying to decide if I should head back to the apartment or book it straight out to see Silas?"

"I think you better head out to Willoughby's place. Things are serious, Mitzy. Definitely give Pyewacket a call, though. He somehow got on that Phoom videoconferencing you had installed and called me."

"Oh no! If he called you, then—"

Hanging up on Erick without saying a proper goodbye is something I'll apologize for later. Letting Silas drive into a trap containing a vengeful Artemis Ward is something I may never get a chance to apologize for.

"Mizithra! How is it you are calling me? Pyewacket assured me you were in grave danger."

Not for the first time, I ponder the true identity of Robin Pyewacket Goodfellow and his pre-cognitive abilities.

"So he called you as well?"

"Indeed. Based on his level of agitation, I was under the impression that Artemis Ward had you under her control."

"Well, that's the cool thing about me, Silas. I'm unpredictable."

Unexpectedly, a belly laugh echoes through the speaker of my phone. "Your penchant for the understatement is a genuine gift."

"Are you at home, Silas?"

"I am not. There was a moment, perhaps five minutes ago, when my search for you bore fruit. Whatever cloaking the sorceress was using to hide you from my view dropped. At that moment, I entered my vehicle and am en route to save you."

"Then you will be proud to know that moment when the cloaking dropped was when I used one of the workings that you taught me to release the ropes that held me to a chair. Then I stole my phone and smashed her altar."

"Impressive. What do you mean, stole your phone?"

"So . . . Did I mention I took a picture of the incantation—?"

"Ah, pity. Unfortunate, but a mistake that any

of us could have made. I'm pleased to hear you have rectified it. However, if she possesses any powers of recall, she may be able to visualize the image from your phone. Your escape was fortuitous. It would appear you've bought us some time. Are you headed to the bookshop?"

"I don't know where to go. I feel lost. I want to let Grams know I'm all right. My dad—"

"I shall meet you at my property. Focus your full attention on driving quickly and safely. I shall phone the necessary parties. Have you heard from Mr. Harper?"

"Yeah, he's all right too. I don't want to put you in any danger, Silas. Maybe I should drive to the airport and get out of town."

"Nonsense. That would only delay the inevitable. You will be safer and better protected at my home. Drive there straightaway."

"Copy that."

Without a mode of transportation, I have no idea how quickly Artemis can launch her pursuit.

The loose end of Alex Crenshaw is also in play. If she's controlling him again, she may have a way to call him to her.

If he's already in Pin Cherry, she may have a way to come after me much sooner than I'd hoped.

The moonlight peeking between branches of the budding birch trees plays hide and seek with me as I approach Silas Willoughby's Gothic mansion.

Taking the hidden right turn, I drive to the rear of the estate, and Silas emerges to greet me.

He holds a fist-sized smoky quartz crystal from a chain and puts up his hand, indicating I must stop where I stand.

"What's wrong? What is that thing?"

"It is similar to a phylactery. Your time with Artemis Ward may have left a residue. Something that she could follow or find."

"Oh. No sweat." Yanking off the goth wig, I scrape my fingers through my hair and smile. "Good as new."

Silas harrumphs. "Not exactly. I must remove all traces before you enter the premises."

Nodding as though this is everyday information, I stand as still as possible while Silas utters a brief Latin phrase and circles the dangling crystal around me counterclockwise from head to toe. When he finishes the working, the crystal is filled with swirling dark energy.

"All of that was on me?"

He nods gravely. "How do you feel?"

Taking a moment to center myself and reach out with my extrasensory abilities, I'm surprised by what I find. "I feel lighter. And cleaner. Does that make sense?"

"Indeed."

Without a word, my mentor walks approximately twenty yards from me, launches the darkened crystal into the air, and it explodes into a mini blizzard of pure-white snowflakes.

"That's one heck of a transmutation. Can you teach me?"

He smiles and smooths his bushy mustache with a thumb and forefinger. "We have more important things to attend to at the moment. Follow me."

For the record, he didn't say no.

Falling in line behind the surprisingly spry alchemist, he leads me to his library. From a secret compartment in the massive oak desk, he extracts a bandolier of supplies. Small vials, crystals, and strange tools are all tucked in neat leather loops spanning the length of the shoulder belt. He slips it over his head and across his chest.

"Place this in your pocket. You'll know when to use it."

It drives me crazy when he gives me instructions like this. Accepting the glass bubble filled with thick purple-blue liquid, I slip it into my pocket and shrug. "I hope you're right."

His gaze fixes on me. The milky cloud that normally covers his eyes has vanished. They are clear blue and exude shocking power. "I am."

CHAPTER 23
ERICK

"Hey, Mitzy, I'm gonna have to let you go. They're wheeling me into surgery. The nurse wants—."

She didn't have time to say goodbye, and I can tell she's worried about me. I can't wait to get this over with and get home. There's a bad feeling in my gut — can't seem to shake it.

The nurse places the phone in the drawstring bag with the rest of my personal items and pushes me into the surgical theater.

"Hello, Mr. Harper. I'm Dr. Sampson. I'll be stitching you up today."

"Thanks, Doc. Folks tell me I've got a pretty hard head, but I guess the skin wasn't as durable as the bone."

"Well, by the time I'm done with you, you'll be

as good as new. I was a board-certified plastic surgeon, back in Florida."

Having lived this far north most of my life, I'm
familiar with people moving *to* Florida to escape the
winter, but not that many come from the other direction. "What pulled you away from the sunshine
and ocean breezes?"

"My wife is a state prison guard. She hit the
glass ceiling, so to speak, in Dade County, and a
better   position   became   available   here   in
Clearwater."

"Understood. How are you doing with the
cold?"

Dr. Sampson chuckles and shrugs his narrow
shoulders. "It was an adjustment. But I honestly
don't miss the heat — or the moneyed Miami
clients. Trauma surgery was my first love when I
started out at Johns Hopkins. I'm happy to be back
at it. And when my elegant sutures can do somebody like you some good. I enjoy that, too."

His easygoing manner is already helping me
relax. "I thought they always say chicks dig scars."

We share a short laugh before Dr. Sampson responds. "They do say that. But in my experience,
they don't dig 'em when they're on the face. Now
the anesthesiologist—"

"Hold up. Don't put me under. I can do this
with a local. I'm not squeamish. In the field, outside

Kandahar, I actually had to stitch up an injured medic."

"Army?"

"Two tours."

"Welcome home, soldier." He turns to the anesthesiologist. "Let's switch the orders to 10cc of lidocaine via subcutaneous infiltration, and we'll get underway."

The anesthesiologist makes the change, checks her syringe, and approaches. "Mr. Harper, you may feel some burning once the lidocaine enters the tissue. Are you sure you'll be all right?"

"Good to go. Squared away."

She leans toward me, and I clench my jaw as she completes the series of numbing injections around the wound.

Dr. Sampson consults with his nurse and checks his surgical kit while he waits for the drug to take effect.

"Are you able to feel this, Mr. Harper?"

"No, sir. Fire when ready."

"My nurse tells me you used to be the sheriff up north. What was the reason for your career change?"

"Same as yours, Doc. A woman."

He laughs lightly, but there is a focus and concentration in his eyes that I admire.

I can feel a little tug here and there, but overall, the experience is pretty painless.

Dr. Sampson steps away, and the nurse cleans me up and places a small bandage over the stitches.

"We'll move you into recovery, Mr. Harper. They'll release you in the morning."

"Just a second." Turning toward the doctor, I fire off the question. "Dr. Sampson, I have someone here to drive me home. Is there any reason why you can't release me immediately?"

The doctor turns, and a grin tugs at one corner of his mouth. "That woman of yours waiting at home for you?"

"You could say that."

"Who's your ride?"

"He actually works over at the state penitentiary. Brian Clark. You heard of him?"

"Sure. I've met Brian a couple times. Is he in the waiting area?"

"I believe so." Whew! I hope he is. Jacob Duncan sounded pretty confident when he claimed he could contact the warden and get Brian Clark's phone number.

The doc nods and exits. Looks like he plans on confirming my story.

"Excuse me, could someone hand me my phone?"

The nurse steps over, takes the phone from the bag, and hands it to me as she checks my bandage.

"Dr. Sampson did an excellent job on your stitches, Mr. Harper. You should definitely follow up with your primary care physician tomorrow. We need to make sure there's no sign of infection."

"10-4."

Dr. Sampson returns. I cross my fingers that it's with good news.

"I spoke to Brian. He's ready and willing to drive you home. Said he got the warden to pull a few strings and get him on the task force saddled with recovering Crenshaw."

My throat tightens as I push myself to a sitting position. The mounting dangers surrounding Mitzy come crashing back. Time to push these emotions down. I've gotten this far through life with the white-knuckle technique. No point changing strategies now.

Dr. Sampson steps forward. "You okay, Harper. You looked pretty green around the gills when you sat up."

"There's a situation unfolding back home. Guess that's hittin' me a little harder than I thought. But as far as the stitches and the accident, I'm all good with that."

He puts a hand on my shoulder and smiles.

"Yeah, the emotions are always harder to deal with than the physical pain. Right?"

Slowly, I get to my feet. Dr. Sampson is only a couple inches shorter than me, but everything feels smaller somehow as I try to wrap my head around what I'll be facing when I get back to Pin Cherry.

The doctor accompanies me to the waiting room. Brian Clark smiles broadly when he catches sight of me. "Looks like I'll be repaying that debt sooner rather than later, eh?"

"I think I'll be the one in your debt after this drive, Clark." Turning, I shake the doctor's hand. "Thanks again, Doc."

Dr. Sampson turns toward Clark and offers a nod that includes us both. "Good luck recovering the escaped convict."

Clark's eyes widen, but he thankfully leaves out the detail of my relationship to Alex Crenshaw.

As we walk toward Clark's late-model Chevy truck, he fills me in on the manhunt. "Local law enforcement issued a BOLO on Crenshaw, and the warden called in a couple of favors to get me on the manhunt. I figured it's no coincidence that you're his only relative, and you live in Pin Cherry Harbor. There might be something to look into once we get up there. I have a stipend to cover meals and whatnot. You guys got a cheap motel up there?"

"I can do you one better, Clark. I still haven't

sold my house. After I got married, I moved into a place my wife and I remodeled together. You can have my house all to yourself. Free of charge."

"Thanks, Harper. I'm starting to feel like my luck changed the moment you walked into that infirmary."

"Happy to help out a fellow lawman."

Clark's four-wheel-drive truck tears up the road. By the time we see the Pin Cherry Harbor city limits sign, my local anesthetic has worn off, and my head is pounding like a death metal drum kit.

"Let's head over to my old place and get you settled." I offer Clark directions and show him where to find the hide-a-key.

"I'll make a quick call to Deputy Gilbert and let him know you're working on the escaped prisoner case — the new one."

He nods his thanks.

I grab the keys to the Nova and send Clark on his way, after promising to let him know if there's any news of Alex Crenshaw.

Clark heads off toward the sheriff's station, and I place a call to Mitzy.

No answer. Again.

This woman is going to be the death of me.

CHAPTER 24

Silas adds a satchel containing two books and canteens of water to our armory.

"Now what? Do we just sit here and wait?"

"The best offense is a good defense."

I don't have the heart to correct Silas. I'll default to Ghost-ma's favorite motto: "You get more flies with honey."

"We know a great deal about Ms. Ward's capabilities, Mizithra, and we have a rough idea regarding her motivations."

I shrug. "Yeah, how does that help us?"

"She has proven she will go to any lengths to get what she wants. A person with such obsessive motivations has a certain weakness."

Warmth surrounds my heart as I adjust my canteen strap. "We can manipulate her. She's more likely to act without thinking, right?"

"Precisely."

With that, Silas exits the library, walks to the back of his large mansion, and stops near the sunroom leading to his magnificent backyard.

The "sun room" is a greenhouse larger than my entire rundown studio apartment back in Arizona. Flowering plants, citrus trees, and fresh vegetables bring life to the space, but the heart-stopping highlight is . . . the view beyond the greenery.

The mansion sits atop a bluff overlooking the great lake, still locked in ice, and for a moment, it's as though I've stepped through a portal to the shores of Wales or Scotland.

"You'll need to switch out your clothing. You must be dressed warmly for this next part of our mission."

Taking one look at the heavy parka, super-insulated winter boots, and woolen mittens shoved inside leather choppers, I become concerned.

"Are we going to be hiking through the freezing cold?"

"Not far, but when we reach our destination, we will be unable to start a fire."

Everything about that explanation makes the muscles in my shoulders tighten. However, I do as

I'm told. I've known Silas Willoughby long enough to understand his judicious use of explanation.

Once we're sufficiently bundled and I've pulled a stocking cap snugly over my ears and wrapped a scarf over my face, we head through the greenhouse.

As we proceed across the slate terrace and down two steps, a chill creeps over my skin, and I hurry to the lowest level of the patio.

It's not until he takes a left at the bottom of the stairs that my chest truly tightens.

"Are we going down to the cave? You think I'm going to survive walking down those narrow stone steps in winter? If that's your plan, we don't need to worry about Artemis! I'll fall to my death long before she ever gets here."

My mentor tromps through the snow and opens the gate, normally hidden by thick ivy in the summer.

I traveled down this stairway once before in my life. It's winding, steep, and not a place for a natural-born klutz.

Silas offers to walk ahead of me, but I flatly refuse. "No way! If I slip and fall to my death, that's on me, but if I slip and fall and knock you off your feet, killing us both — that's not something I can live with."

My logical and practical mentor smooths his

bushy grey mustache and harrumphs. "If you were to fall to your death, Mizithra, my demise would hardly be something you'd have to live with."

Blerg. He's right, but that doesn't mean I have to like it.

He heads down the narrow steps like one of those corkscrew-horned goats in the Himalayas. I follow more slowly, testing each footing before placing my full weight on the descending leg and sliding my mittened hand along the rock face for balance.

A frigid wind knifing across the great lake does us no favors. Tears are freezing to my eyelashes, and I can't feel my face. And trust me when I tell you, that's not a hook to a pop song; that's reality.

At long last, we reach the bottom of the staircase, and we're forced to pick our way across the narrow strip of snow-covered shore. Mounds of ice push up against each other, creating strange shapes. The pale setting sun makes no effort to penetrate the frozen monuments.

Silas leads the way to the hidden cave I once explored before selling pickles at a Ren Faire, but that's another story.

"What's our move here, Silas? If we wait for Artemis to find us, there's no way out. And I'm useless. I can't help you. At least let me head somewhere else and serve as bait for—"

A stomping outside the entrance of the cave stabs fear through my heart. I shove my hand in the pocket of the parka to retrieve the glass ball.

Blast it!

Silas steps forward. "Welcome, Nimkii. I was not sure you would answer the call."

Nimkii pulls up the ski mask covering his face and walks toward us. But before he can offer his greeting, I blurt in panic, "Silas, I left the bubble thing you gave me in my other coat. Plus, my phone is up there!"

Silas gestures for me to be patient.

Yeesh. He really knows how to get me.

The calm Native American man steps forward and shakes my mentor's hand. "I will always answer the call, dear friend. What do we face this evening? Is this a creature of the animal world, the human world, or the spirit world?"

Silas unzips his thick coat and reveals part of the bandolier. "On this night, we face a creature of the human world fueled by stolen spirits."

Nimkii's brow creases, and he shakes his head. "We must contact the ancestors and request their help."

Silas nods once. "Indeed."

To be fair, I feel lost in the presence of this powerful alchemist and the equally talented shaman.

"Should I run back up to the house and get my phone and—"

Silas turns, and the mere touch of his gaze silences me. "It is best that you have forgotten your phone. As for the vial, it was little more than a party trick. A distraction which may have offered you escape. I have other tools on which we may rely."

Nimkii steps beside Silas. For the first time, I notice how similar they look. Approximately the same height, both unassuming in their daily life, but when faced with true tribulation, the power emanating from the men is extraordinary.

"What can I do? I have to help. We have to make sure she doesn't take anyone else."

The shaman produces a palm-size deerskin bag stained with something I'm not sure I want to ask about.

"We can bind the power in here, Willoughby. Did you perfect the funnel?"

Now they seem to be speaking their own private language, like fraternal twins. I'm on the outside. Helpless.

"Mizithra. You are familiar with setting the circle for a séance. We must call on the ancestors. Nimkii will petition his people. I will call Jedediah, Rivail, and Penny — if they are able to answer. However, you must call your mother."

"My mother? She wasn't a witch or an alchemist. What can my mother do?"

Silas steps forward, removes his glove, and places his hand on my cheek. "She can protect you. Perhaps more effectively than all the alchemy in the universe."

Behind him, Nimkii nods reverently and mumbles, "The Queen's gambit." Silas nods once as he hands me the chalk, candles, and a large labradorite crystal.

"What's the Queen's gambit, Silas?" There's no possible way my fusty mentor is referring to the pop culture hit mini-series. "I remember the names of the chess pieces, and I know that's some kind of move. Am I the Queen?"

Silas remains motionless, but a ragged breath shakes his chest. Nimkii looks away from me.

There are moments when I wish I wasn't psychic. I will remember this painful moment for the rest of my life — assuming it lasts beyond tonight.

"You're the Queen, aren't you, Silas? If you mean to sacrifice yourself to save me, I won't allow it. I will not allow another person to die protecting me. I'm not sure what you all think I'm capable of, but whatever it is, you're wrong. I'm just a carnival psychic who's solved a few crimes. I refuse to let you give your life for me."

Silas turns away from me and whispers softly, "Prepare the circle for the séance."

The temperature inside the cave is biting cold, although not nearly as frigid as the frosty wind in the open air.

As I draw the pentacle on the stone slab and set the candles, my tears fall silently to the granite.

Placing the large labradorite crystal in the center of the pentacle, I turn to the two elders. "Did I do it right?"

Silas steps toward me and hands me a small vial. "Keeping the points of the pentagram inside the circle of the pentacle is correct for this working. Here is a tincture of mugwort, yarrow, angelica, rue, and mandrake. Pour it over the crystal and place the empty vial in your pocket."

Once again, I do as I'm told.

The moment I finish anointing the crystal—

A bolt of heat seems to rocket from the granite through the bottoms of my feet and explode from the top of my head. "Silas!"

He and Nimkii turn, take one look at me, and rush into the pentacle.

"What do you see?"

Silas helps me to take a seat on one side of the crystal while he and Nimkii take up the other two points of a triangle. We all join hands as a strange vision unfolds.

"I'm running down a snowy road. I'm filled with rage."

Silas squeezes my hand. "This is not you, Mizithra. You are experiencing sight beyond sight. Did you touch the Eye of the Priestess?"

"Maybe?" My psychic recall of that moment is sketchy. "I wiped my arm across the altar, knocking everything to the floor. I might've touched it. Why?"

"I fear Artemis Ward has successfully performed the incantation. The veil that protects us has dropped, but because you touched the eye, the cloak that hid her from our view has also fallen. You are able to see what she sees."

"Doesn't that mean she could see what I'm—"

Silas grips my hand firmly. "Close your eyes."

Immediately, my eyelids slam closed. I can only hope that she hasn't realized our connection.

"We must move forward with the séance, Mizithra. Keep your eyes closed. Forget about Artemis Ward. She is on her way to us. She will find us. All we can do now is prepare for her arrival."

A surge of power courses through us in a clockwise motion.

Nimkii begins with a call to his ancestors in his native tongue. The rhythm has a flow and clip that is mesmerizing, and I can feel supportive energy circling around us.

Silas picks up the chant and, in a combination of Latin, possibly Greek, and definitely Polish, he calls the spirits of his fallen friends to the circle. Surprisingly, I feel the energy of Ania Karina join us, and I hope I live long enough to tell Tadjo about his brave mother.

Silas squeezes my hand, and now it's my turn.

The ritual of the makeup from my childhood. That's the one connection that always puts me closest to Coraline Moon. Working through each step, I picture my mother's face clearly, hearing her voice and her sweet British accent as though she were right beside me. I speak the ending line of the memory: "Then she would apply a little mascara to my lashes before she coated her own and finish by saying, 'Dark lashes give you a finished look. Serious but mysterious.' And she would kiss the tip of my nose."

In an instant, the hairs on the back of my neck spike, and warmth creeps across my shoulders. "She's here."

Silas draws my hands to the center, and I want to open my eyes. However, I don't want Artemis to have even an inkling of what we're doing.

He places my hands on the crystal and offers a final instruction. "Do not release your hold on the crystal. Nimkii and I will vacate the circle and draw the spirits with us. Your mother's energy shall remain with you. She'll protect you. You must hold within the safety of the circle while I handle Artemis Ward." He sighs heavily.

I believe in Silas with all my heart, but this day is darker than I ever could've imagined.

My husband is somewhere between a hospital and Pin Cherry Harbor, my grandmother has no idea what's transpired, and my mentor is willing to die to save me . . .

I can't imagine anything that could turn the tides in our favor.

"RE-OW!" Game on!

CHAPTER 25

THE RAPTURE of hearing Pyewacket join the team sends my spirits soaring. The elation barely lasts ten seconds.

"I can't believe you were all so easy to find."

At the gloating sound of Artemis Ward's voice, my eyes pop open in dismay.

She's all business. Her long curls are pulled into a high ponytail and— Is that a tattoo on her neck?

Her sparkling violet-blue eyes lock on to me in a second, and her mocking tone echoes off the cold cave walls. "Did you really think that closing your eyes like a misinformed toddler could stop me? Perhaps you're not nearly the prize I'd hoped. Object permanence exists on more planes than the visual. I would've thought your self-important mentor would have covered that in Magic 101." She crosses her arms and inhales sharply.

"It's alchemy!" Me and my big mouth. Like semantics is our biggest issue right now.

My mother's glowing spirit stirs as Silas and Nimkii adjust their positions to place themselves between me and the advancing dark energy of Artemis Ward.

She lifts her hands and electricity crackles at her fingertips.

Silas rises to his full height and spins one hand over the other as he whispers, "Trąba powietrzna."

A tornado forms within the cave and then swirls violently around Artemis Ward.

Initially, she's thrown off balance, and whatever magic she had been summoning is put to an immediate halt.

Nimkii opens the bag as Silas offers an additional command. The swirling winds shift from a vertical cyclone to something more horizontal, funneling into Nimkii's precious container.

Sadly, their true purpose dawns on me seconds later than Artemis.

She falls to one knee, placing both her hands on the granite cave floor.

The swirling wind seems to be sucked into the very stone itself.

Artemis rises and slings a bolt of fiery energy toward Nimkii.

The native elder easily dodges the attack, but the sacred bag ignites into a ball of flame. He's forced to drop the pouch, as the spirits of his ancestors surge toward the intruder.

From my vantage point within the protective circle, I can't be sure if Artemis can see the approaching spirits or simply sense them. Either way, she conjures a protective shield around her space.

Silas traces a series of three sigils into the air, as though it were a solid substance.

Her shield vanishes, and the spirits descend.

The apparition of Ania Karina joins the fray, and my eyes nearly pop out of my head as I watch her attempt to disappear into the being of Artemis Ward.

Some type of possession.

Pyewacket continues to pace around me, outside the circle. He seems to have appointed himself as the last line of defense.

The physical form of Artemis Ward takes on a dark shimmering hue, and Ania Karina's spirit is propelled backward.

The ghost's thick Polish accent calls out in shock. "The mark on your neck! It can't be!"

I await Artemis Ward's reply, but none comes. Looks like confirmation that she can't see or hear the spirits — only sense their energy. Maybe I can use that to my advantage. Vengeful spirits seem more threatening than confused ghosts.

"Remember that Polish woman you killed in the Emporium? Her vengeful spirit wants to know about the marking on your neck. Is it a tattoo?"

The shimmering darkness softens, and Artemis scoffs. "Never. It's a horrid birthmark. I tried to remove it several times. It's impenetrable."

Ania Karina swirls toward me. "It's the broken crescent. It's not possible. The doctor told me my daughter died."

Gripping the large labradorite crystal in my hands, I stand and drop my truth bomb. "The mother you were searching for is dead — by your own hand. You betrayed your family in your lust for power. Your twisted magic has left you with nothing."

Ms. Ward's eyes blaze with fury. "That woman was not my family. She was the means to an end. An unhinged doctor stole me at birth. When I escaped that woman's clutches at fifteen, I dedicated my life to the pursuit of magical truth."

My mentor's voice booms through the low-ceilinged cave, and bits of rock and debris sprinkle down from above. "Murder is not truth!"

"That blood is on your hands, fool. If you hadn't built a society of secrets to hide my true mother from me, I would've been able to access the information I needed — without resorting to such extreme measures!"

"The society had nothing to do with your origins. Your existence was unknown to us." There's a hard edge to Mr. Willoughby's voice. Almost as though he's angry with himself for missing the signs that may have pointed to Artemis sooner.

The spirit of Tadjo's mother begins to fade. Power once again crackles at the fingertips of the sorceress.

"Wait! Mrs. Nowak is trying to speak."

Silas and Nimkii slowly back away from Artemis. There's still a subtle glow in her hands, but nothing active.

"Mrs. Nowak insists she was told the baby died. She doesn't believe this woman's lies." I can't get a read off Artemis, so I'm no help in confirming or disproving the claim.

Artemis draws an athamé from her belt, and Silas instantly lifts his hand to counter the attack.

"Don't worry, old man. I only wish to show this alleged ghost the truth of my claim." Artemis takes the tip of her dagger and pricks her index finger. As a ruby bubble rises on her flesh, she challenges the spirit. "With all of your power, knowledge, and the information you can access in the afterlife, you can certainly verify my claim." Artemis raises her hand in the air, clearly not able to see the ghost of Ania Karina. "Tell me, am I your blood?"

The spirit of Mrs. Nowak moves toward the outstretched hand, and as her energy swirls around the wound, she gasps and succumbs to a lifetime of pent-up tears.

Artemis glances my direction. "Well, what does she say?"

"It's true, Silas. Artemis is Mrs. Nowak's biological daughter. Annie Spuścizna Nowak."

Silas whispers, "Once a legacy, now a tragedy tainted by evil."

The ghost of Mrs. Nowak glances toward me, presses a hand to her heart, and vanishes. Whatever drew her through the veil, whatever power compelled her to join our fight, has vanished.

I'll keep that information to myself as long as I can. Unfortunately, I've been in this situation enough times to know that keeping the bad guy, or in this case gal, talking is in our best interest.

"Artemis, did the woman who kidnapped you give you that name?"

"That woman was clueless and mundane." She scoffs and continues, "After I left for good, I chose my own name. The goddess of wild animals. Artemis. I chose the name Ward as a reminder that I would be no one's possession for the rest of my life — and also as a warning to those who may trifle with me. Promising myself I wouldn't rest until I had recovered my ancestor's grimoire and everything that was taken from me." Her fists ball at her sides and energy crackles around her knuckles. "Some magic force pulled me to the Emporium. I never meant to hurt the gypsy. I only wanted what I thought she'd taken from my family."

As I open my mouth to respond, Silas takes the baton. "The true error is that you've taken many things that did not belong to you, Miss Ward."

"You've been warned, wizard." Energy sparks from her fingertips and knocks Silas backward.

Pyewacket launches into action.

His lightning-fast reflexes give him a slight advantage. He's able to seriously wound her arm before bounding back toward me.

"Good one, Pye."

"Ree-OW!" A warning punctuated by a threat.

Silas gets to his feet with surprising speed.

Artemis changes tactics.

Using her powers to temporarily cloak herself, she slips past my mentor and Nimkii. Perhaps because of my brief contact with the Eye of the Priestess, she remains visible to me the entire time.

As she slinks toward me, her lips move wordlessly, and even an amateur such as myself can tell she's stirring up a dangerous spell.

Silas launches a gust of wind that lifts her invisibility, knocks her off her feet, and sends her rolling toward the back of the cave.

"Mizithra, take the crystal and run." It's not a request.

Fairly sure my actions aren't my own, I feel compelled to grip the crystal tightly and bolt toward the cave's exit.

Pyewacket remains.

As I stumble up the narrow stairway toward the mansion above, a sick heaviness in my stomach emerges as I worry I may never see Silas, Nimkii, or Pyewacket again.

Nope. I push that from my mind.

The climb is exhausting, and my mother's energy could not leave the séance circle.

I'm alone. Exhausted. And—

Strong arms grip me, and, for a moment, I dare to hope Erick has come to my rescue.

However, the voice that threatens me is not what I had hoped for.

Alex Crenshaw wrenches my arm behind my back, sending the labradorite crystal careening down the staircase. Smashing into a hundred bits.

Exactly like my heart.

He holds a gun to my side as he forces me down the stairs. "Don't do anything stupid. Artemis won't be happy until she has what she came for."

I'd love to tell him that the grimoire she seeks is

locked in a vault beyond my reach, but I've already made too many mistakes on this case. If I can protect that grimoire, at least I can die with a shred of dignity.

When Alex Crenshaw shoves me through the low opening into the cave, an epic battle is in play.

The spirits of the ancestors, plus Rivail, Penny, and Jedediah, have encircled Artemis Ward and are redirecting the energy of her curses.

Silas is wounded, and somehow Nimkii is sharing energy with him so he can re-create the alchemical funnel needed to drain Artemis Ward of her ill-gotten powers.

Nimkii has a burn on his left leg, and without his sacred bag, I'm not sure where he can trap these powers.

Alex Crenshaw's voice rings out. "Release Artemis at once, or I'll put a bullet in your prodigy."

I hadn't noticed it earlier, because he caught me off guard, but his voice is wavering and unsteady. There's a hollow echo to his words, almost as though he were a ventriloquist dummy—

"Drop the gun, Crenshaw. Let go of the girl and back away."

Once again, the voice I had hoped would be Erick's, instead belongs to an unfamiliar balding man with a thick brown mustache.

Crenshaw pivots toward the new threat and backs against the cave wall to limit his exposure.

"Don't come any closer, Clark. I mean it—"

The hairs on the back of my neck stand on end, and my tummy lurches.

Somewhere deep in my psychic senses, I feel Alex struggling to resist. Maybe his claims were true . . .

What if Artemis Ward is more powerful than any of us imagined?

CHAPTER 26
ERICK

As I DUCK under the rock overhang and step into the cave behind Brian Clark, I feel as though I've entered a world of pure imagination — nightmares come to life.

My biological father is holding a gun to my wife's head.

A woman probably responsible for forcing him to commit murder has electricity crackling from her hands like a villain in a superhero movie, and Nimkii, the man I grew up sharing a fishing boat with, has somehow been involved in whatever Silas Willoughby is doing.

I have never been more out of my depth.

Better fall back on my training. Pick a target. It's gotta be Alex Crenshaw.

"Erick, wait—"

The concern on Mitzy's face doesn't make sense. The man is holding a gun to her head, and somehow she's worried about him.

Maybe I can convince him to give up his hostage. "Drop the gun, Crenshaw. No one else—"

Electricity fires across the cave. My battle instincts kick in, and I duck for cover.

Unfortunately, Brian Clark takes the hit and sprawls onto the granite. His gun bounces across the rocks like a stone skipping on a pond.

Willoughby does something I won't even try to explain, and Artemis Ward crumples against the cave wall.

Looking toward Crenshaw, I see an opening. The sequence of events distracted him, and his aim has wavered. The gun is no longer pointed directly at Mitzy's head. If I take the shot—

"No!" Mitzy angles her body in front of Alex Crenshaw.

In all the years I've known her, I've seen her risk her life for the most ridiculous reasons. But if she thinks I'm gonna let her die to save a murderer, she doesn't know me nearly as well as she thinks.

Artemis Ward stirs, and Pyewacket makes his move.

He lunges at the woman, bites hard on a velvet

pouch hanging from her belt, yanks it free, and runs for Willoughby.

Steadying my aim, I attempt to thread the needle above my wife's left shoulder and into the larger target of Alex Crenshaw behind her.

That's when I see it.

That's when I understand what my amazing wife has known for the last ten minutes — at least.

The look on Crenshaw's face is one of agony. He doesn't want to hurt anyone. He's trying to drop the gun, but his own hand isn't responding.

Pyewacket delivers the small velvet pouch to Silas, and no matter how many times I relive this moment, I'll never believe what I see.

The elderly lawyer holds the bag in one hand as it bursts into yellow-orange flame. He pulls something from one of the hidden pockets of his ancient tweed coat, and as he pours it into the flames, red sparks shoot from the burning mass in his left hand.

There's an — explosion. That's the only way I can describe it.

When the dust settles, Alex Crenshaw is curled into a fetal position on the ground just behind Mitzy.

At the spot where I'd seen Artemis Ward only seconds before, there's nothing but a pile of ash.

. . .

Mitzy is crawling toward me with tears streaming down her face.

When she reaches me, I slide across the rock and pull her close, as I wipe dust from my eyes and get my bearings.

Nimkii is rubbing his head and attempting to sit up.

"Nimkii, you good?"

He turns slowly toward me and shrugs with extreme nonchalance. "I may need a poultice for my leg. But I can walk, eh?"

Whatever has happened to Alex Crenshaw has locked him in silence. I can deal with that later. Dragging Mitzy with me, we crawl toward Silas Willoughby.

Pyewacket reaches him first.

The brave caracal presses his broad forehead against Silas and shoves.

There's no response.

Reaching Willoughby a moment after Mitzy, I roll him onto his back and check for a pulse.

If there is one, it's too faint for me to feel with my fingers.

"Erick, he's going to be all right. Right? I'm sure you've seen worse."

All I can think is, *seen worse?* I've never seen anything like this in my entire life. For Mitzy's sake, I nod and attempt a smile.

Before I can formulate an actual answer, Pyewacket climbs onto Willoughby's chest and pushes his whiskered face close to the fallen lawyer's mouth and nose.

The events of this night will never make sense to me.

Mitzy removes her mother's dreamcatcher necklace from around her neck and gently slips it over Willoughby's head.

Pyewacket places his paw on the crystal in the center of the weaving, and I swear to you, it glows a brilliant purple.

Nimkii moves closer, and Mitzy says the strangest thing. "The ancestors have departed. Jedediah is still here."

The shaman nods and extracts a leather thong from his pocket. Next, he ties his own wrist to Willoughby's left wrist.

He begins a deep chant. The violet glow in the crystal grows, and soon, the cave is bathed in royal light.

Willoughby gasps as though he's surfaced from a deep ocean dive.

Pyewacket collapses and rolls onto the stone.

Mitzy surges forward and cradles Silas in her arms. I place my hand under the wild cat's head and pray he's alive. For her sake.

"Silas! Silas, talk to me." Tears trickle from her soft cheeks to her mentor's dusty coat.

A weak voice greets her. "Mizithra. Good of you to stay. I must admit, I could do with a cup of tea."

My wife laughs through her tears.

Brian Clark rubs his head and moans.

Gently releasing Pyewacket, I run to Clark's side, and help him to a sitting position as he gazes around the cave in wonder. "What happened? I feel like I got tased, but like real bad."

The truth can never leave these walls, so I start building the best story I can. "Yeah, you definitely got tased. Why don't you put Crenshaw in cuffs and head up? I'll make sure everyone else is okay, and we'll follow with Artemis Ward. Good job, Clark. You got your man. The warden owes you a promotion."

Luckily, the prison guard is still disoriented enough to buy what I'm selling.

Clark scrabbles across the hard rock, handcuffs Crenshaw, and propels him out of the cave. "I'm taking this guy straight back to Clearwater, Harper."

"10-4." A tiny piece of me wants to stop the prison guard, but there's no way to explain what I think I understand. If I want to help Crenshaw, I'll need evidence. As Mitzy would say, that's a job for future me.

As soon as Clark leaves, I turn to the others. "Would one of you mind telling me what's going on? What happened to Artemis Ward?"

Silas struggles to a seated position and leans against Mitzy. "Ah, this is a tale to tell over break-fast, Mr. Harper. If you could assist me to my feet, I must complete our business."

Not understanding what he's talking about, I help the old man up.

Willoughby and Nimkii approach the pile of ash as though it were a coiled cobra.

"Mizithra, the key to Bell, Book & Candle, please."

My shaken but brave wife slips the large brass key from around her neck and passes it to her mentor.

Willoughby grips the crystal dangling around his neck, pushes it through the opening at the top of the strange triangular key, and draws symbols in the air like a child finger-painting on an invisible canvas.

The pile of ash begins to swirl.

Instinctively, I pull Mitzy behind me.

For once, she stays put. Her arms circle around my waist, and I feel a flood of relief.

Nimkii opens a small beaded pouch made of

buckskin. The only reason I know that it's buckskin is because I remember seeing it, ages ago, displayed in his hunting cabin.

He told me the story of finding the wounded buck deep in the woods. Some hunter had winged the animal and then abandoned the hunt. Nimkii claimed the animal spoke to him and offered his pelt in exchange for an end to his suffering.

I was young, and, at the time, didn't believe in the paranormal. I remember thinking it was an interesting story, but didn't pay attention to the details. Now, as I stare at the precious bag, an entire hidden world unravels in my brain.

The pile of ash swirls toward the opening in the bag. Once every bit has been contained, Nimkii ties off the neck of the bag with the leather thong that had previously bound his wrist to Willoughby's.

The two men embrace, and Silas takes the ceremonial bag from his friend.

"Let us return to my home. I must place this in the vault, and then I shall set about creating a celebratory breakfast worthy of the night's events."

I motion for him and Nimkii to take the lead.

Mitzy follows, clutching the unconscious caracal to her chest.

As I support her and her burden, we carefully climb the treacherous stairs.

With each breath of the fresh air, I swear I can feel spring emerging.

When we reach the gate, an earsplitting crack echoes across the great lake, and all heads turn.

Nimkii's sharp eyes glisten. "The thaw."

CHAPTER 27

"Silas, Pyewacket is going to be all right, isn't he?"

"Indeed. Do not underestimate his strength, Mizithra. He is fortunate that the universe reset the tally when he gave his ninth life to save Isadora. I believe this sacrifice he made so recently may have cost a heavy price. Let us assume he has seven lives remaining."

As I stroke the broad tan head of my furry overlord, I nearly squeal when his black tufted ears twitch.

"Mr. Cuddlekins, you're all right! You want some Fruity Puffs?"

"Reow." Can confirm. The tone is unusually quiet, but the message is clear.

Silas whips up breakfast for the boys, while I raid his pantry for the stash of sugary children's cereal I know he maintains. It was no accident that Pyewacket knew his way to my mentor's Gothic mansion.

The bond that exists between this mysterious caracal and my wise mentor seems to span more than one lifetime.

The more I learn about Robin Pyewacket Good-fellow, the more I believe the carving of his exact like-ness that exists on the three-hundred-year-old front door of my bookshop is no accident or coincidence.

Pyewacket has many secrets. I doubt I'll live nearly enough lifetimes to discover them all.

"Breakfast is served." The still-weak voice of Silas Willoughby calls us to the table.

"Smells amazing! Don't tell Odell." Erick and Nimkii chuckle.

"I shall join you presently. I have business to which I must attend."

Silas takes the leather pouch containing the ashes of Artemis Ward and disappears toward his library.

Following him into the wide hall, I call softly, "Silas, what happened to Artemis? If she's ashes, why is she still dangerous?"

He harrumphs and speaks without turning. "The powers Artemis stole from Rivail and Penny had been tainted by her darkness. Nimkii and I separated her from her powers, and the crystal key pulled the light from the darkness. These ashes contain the most twisted energies of Artemis Ward. They must be locked away forever."

"What about the powers?" I step toward him.

Silas turns in the dim hallway, his eyes glowing clear blue. "You are not ready."

Gasping, I step back. "What? Oh, no. I wasn't . . . I just wanted my key back."

A throaty guffaw breaks the tension. "Of course." He slips the key from one of his hidden inner pockets and presses it into my hand. "You did well, Mizithra."

Gulp. "Thanks." Taking the key, I shove it in my pocket and hurry back to Erick.

When Silas returns, he holds the grimoire of Mrs. Nowak.

"Now that the threat of Artemis Ward has been removed, I believe Mrs. Nowak wished you to study this material."

"Yeah, but I don't have a vault. How can I keep it safe?" I shrug.

"Despite the threats of our most recent rival, secrecy will be your friend. If you can keep from mentioning its whereabouts, none will be the wiser."

"What? Seems pretty sus-spish. Aren't you the

one who's always preaching honesty as the best defense?"

"I have come to realize that one can hold both ideals in balance. What matters is discernment. Learning to identify each situation accurately. You possess exceptional gifts, Mizithra. It is no accident that this grimoire has been given to you."

"I'll take your word for it, Silas. Now, if I don't eat something, I will literally faint."

A general round of laughter ensues, as we all dig into fluffy, purple, ube pancakes, topped with fresh bananas and maple whipped cream.

Oh, and coffee — loads of coffee!

CHAPTER 28

NORMALLY, solving a case is cause for celebration. This one feels different. A man I now consider my friend, Tadjo, lost a mother and a sister in a bizarre paranormal sequence of events. There's no bad guy to put in jail, and the unpleasant task of attending a funeral looms on the horizon.

As the gang gathers in my old apartment, the job of updating Grams falls squarely on my shoulders.

"It was an epic battle, Grams. The kind I'd normally be super pumped to tell you about, but we came so close to losing Silas — and Pyewacket!" My voice catches in my throat.

"Oh, sweetie! I can't believe what you've all been through. And you're sure this Artemis Ward woman is truly the long-lost— *was* truly the long-lost daughter of Ania Karina?"

I inhale sharply. "Every fiber of my psychic being confirms it."

Erick leans forward as he adjusts his weight in the scalloped-back chair. "What are we going to do about Alex Crenshaw?"

"No idea. It's not like you can approach a judge or the parole board with the truth. Who's going to believe that a powerful sorceress manipulated your father— sorry — Alex into killing two people so she could absorb their powers?"

"Yeah. I don't even believe it myself."

Grams zooms down from her floaty perch near the ceiling. "Mitzy, what if she didn't?"

My shocked grey eyes nearly pop out of my head. "Grams! I've seen her powers. I'm sure she was manipulating Crenshaw."

"That's not what I meant, dear. Oh goodness! The thought of losing Pye has me all in a jumble." She clutches a strand of her pearls and chokes back a ghost sob.

"Silas is taking care of Pyewacket. I'm not sure exactly what happened in those caverns below his gothic mansion, but whatever it was, I know Silas will make it right." I nod to affirm my statement.

Grams breathes a sigh of relief, but before she can finish her previous thought, Erick interrupts.

"Yeah, good thing we have Silas. Those injuries aren't exactly something we could explain to Doc Ledo or any of his vet techs, right?"

"You're really getting the hang of this supernatural mischief, aren't you, Harper?"

A weary grin lifts his rugged cheeks. "I guess I am. At the risk of repeating myself, glad you're on my team, Moon."

"Same here." Turning my attention back to Ghost-ma, I attempt to get her back on track. "So, what were you trying to say about Alex Crenshaw?"

Grams blinks, and her glowing eyes rove back and forth for a moment before she responds. "Oh! Right. I remember an exercise that Penny used to practice when she was part of the coven. It had to do with absorbing the healing properties of various herbs so that one could use those powers to heal another. It was incredibly complicated, and not something I pursued, but I remember exactly how Penny explained the process. She had a special crescent-moon-charged boline knife that she used to cut a plant from its main stock. It was at the moment she severed the shoot from its life-giving roots that she could absorb the powers. So—"

Leaping to my feet, a wave of realization washes over me. "I get it! There's no way Alex Crenshaw could've done this. If Artemis wanted to absorb the powers of Penny and Rivail, she would've had to commit these crimes herself. I'll check with Silas, but I think you're onto something, Grams."

She lifts the skirt of her Marchesa gown and makes a small curtsy. Of course, the gesture draws attention to the torn hem, and she winces with thoughts of what her poor dress has endured.

Erick drags his left thumb along his stubbled jaw. "Are you saying there could be a legitimate chance Alex Crenshaw didn't kill those people?"

I nod like a bobblehead doll on a car dashboard. "Like I said, I'll have to check with Silas — when he's feeling better, of course — but what Grams said makes sense."

He smiles. "And what exactly did she say?"

Oops. Looks like I ignored my side hustle as an afterlife interpreter. As I bring Erick up to speed, a smile forms and pieces fall into place for him. Even the smallest chance that his father isn't a cold-blooded killer brings him comfort.

"We better get some sleep before tomorrow, Ricky."

My husband pulls his gaze from a faraway place and tilts his head. "What's tomorrow?"

"Mrs. Nowak's funeral. I promised Tadjo we'd be there."

In a flash, he's by my side, brushing the hair back from my face. "Are you sure you're up to that?

You've been through a lot. And I'm not just talking about tonight."

Leaning into him, I inhale his citrus-woodsy scent. "I can do it. I want to be there to support Tadjo. And I feel like I owe that to their family. I'm not sure if he told his brother or his father about Ania Karina leaving me the grimoire, but that sorta makes it feel like we're all part of the same family now. That matters, don't you think?"

"Yeah, I think you're right about that." Casting his gaze around the room, Erick addresses the ghost he can't see. "Thanks for giving me a sliver of hope, Isadora. I gotta get this one into bed. Good night."

Despite the seriousness of the situation, Grams snickers at the mention of bed.

"Good night, Grams. Get your mind out of the gutter."

She winks at me and swirls off toward the closet as she calls over her shimmering shoulder, "You know we both grew from the same trollop tree, dear. Don't get too high and mighty."

AS THE HEARSE PULLS AWAY from the sleet-soaked curb, I lean into the circle of safety beneath the umbrella Erick holds above our heads. Heavy chunks of frozen rain drop on the nylon fabric and slide, unfettered, to the ground.

He shifts the umbrella from one hand to the other and slips an arm around my shoulders. "I know this is hard for you, Moon. What's going through your head right now?"

The scared foster kid inside me doesn't want to let her guard down. I only have a smattering of disconnected memories from my mother's funeral. When Coraline Moon was taken from me, I was too young to fully understand how that would affect my childhood.

But I grew up quickly and hardened my shell as I careened headlong through a tumultuous six-and-a-half years in foster care.

At least Ania Karina's sons are grown men. Hopefully, they're better equipped.

Erick squeezes me and whispers, "We don't have to go to the cemetery if you're not up for it. I got your back. Whatever you decide."

And then the tears fall.

The worst thing anyone can do when I'm upset is to be nice to me. Pick a fight, call me names — that's all fine and good. I'll simply double down on my defenses. But if you're nice? That's when my walls collapse.

Erick kisses the top of my head and steers us toward the Nova. As we gaze toward the funeral procession — a black hearse, Mr. Nowak senior's beat-up pickup truck, and Tadjo's BMW carrying both brothers — I find a kernel of inner strength. "It's all right. We can go to the cemetery. There were so few of us at the service . . . I can't leave Tadjo and his brother alone at the graveside. Especially after having to break the news about Artemis Ward being their sister. Yeesh!" Raking my hand through my hair, I exhale with extra force. "I can pull it together."

My wonderful husband eases into the short row of cars slinking out toward the cemetery where my grandmother is buried, but thankfully, does not reside.

As we arrive, the caretaker and the two men from the funeral home assist Tadjo and Ray in transporting the casket to the graveside. A pop-up tent beside the seemingly bottomless hole in the earth stands alone on the grounds. Just one service today. Just the one loss.

The priest from the family's Eastern Orthodox church must have ridden in the truck with Mr. Nowak. He steps under the protection of the pop-up tent, and we all close our umbrellas to join him.

The film-school dropout in me longs for the umbrellas to remain open. A mournful drone shot, passing over the umbrellas and pulling back to reveal the cemetery . . . But in real life, there's nothing poetic or cinematographic about putting a casket in the ground.

Heartbreaking. Final. Joyless.

Tadjo steps closer and grips my hand.

The tears rolling down his cheeks are all too real. I squeeze his fingers and fruitlessly attempt to blink back my own fresh onslaught.

Ray, the older brother, has hands shoved deep into the pockets of his raincoat and his jaw seems set in stone. His eyes are dry, and he stares straight ahead. Desperate to hold it together.

Words are spoken, the casket is lowered, and the sons step forward, each of them letting fall a single white snowdrop bloom into their mother's grave.

Mr. Nowak nods perfunctorily at the priest and returns to his truck.

Turning to Tadjo, I offer him a hug, and he readily accepts. Ray nods at me over his younger brother's shoulder, much the same way as their father acknowledged the clergy.

We part company, Erick pops up our umbrella, and we walk in silence to our car.

"You did everything you could, Moon."

"I know. I wish things had turned out differently with Artemis . . . Some people can't be saved."

He reaches across the car and squeezes my knee. "It's the hardest lesson I've ever had to learn." He swallows and draws a ragged breath. "Tadjo will need a friend, and he's lucky to have you."

And the tears are falling again.

"I need french fries, Harper. Stat."

He smiles and puts us on a direct course for Myrtle's Diner.

As I step through that doorway, the warm, deep-brown eyes of Odell meet mine across the black-and-white checkered linoleum floor. My heart swells with love.

My mother's death was horrible, and I will never stop missing her, but something good grew out of all of that. Sure, it took almost ten years for Silas Willoughby to track me down, but the life I have here in Pin Cherry Harbor is one in a million. Maybe I can help Tadjo find some kind of silver lining in all of this.

As we slide into the booth, I glance around to find my favorite red-haired waitress, but Tally is nowhere to be found. Odell pops out of the kitchen and offers half a smile. In one hand, he holds a huge platter of beautiful golden french fries and, in the other, two mugs of coffee.

When he slides the items onto the table, I look up and smile. "I'd ask how you knew, but we both know the psychic nut didn't fall far from the tree. Right, Gramps?"

He places a hand on my shoulder and gives me a comforting squeeze. "I'm glad you did right by Mrs. Nowak. Plenty of folks in this town were happy to run to her when they had a problem, but none of them could be bothered to pay their respects, could they?"

"You're right, Gramps. Just family, plus me and Erick, at the service. Do you think it matters how many people attend your funeral?"

An unexpected chuckle escapes his lips as he leans back and rakes his weathered hand through his white-gray buzz cut. "Depends on who you ask. I think the people who care about you will be there . . . That's all that matters to me. Now, if you ask Isadora . . ." He raps his knuckles twice on the silver-flecked Formica table and returns to the kitchen.

Erick walks his fingers across the table and turns his palm up. As I slide my hand into his, he rubs his thumb along the back of my knuckles and smiles. "I think it matters how you treat people when you're alive. If you care about someone or someone cares about you, they should make the effort to see you when you're still breathing. I'm not going to be too impressed when my long-lost friends or relatives show up to throw a spoonful of dirt on my grave."

"Copy that, Harper. Sounds like it's time to send Gracie Harper another airline ticket. What do you think about that?"

He squeezes my fingers. "Thank you. You're

the best wife a guy could ask for. And if we book her tickets for the end of May, it might actually be warm enough for her up here. I'll take care of it."

"Please do. I have to maintain my world's greatest daughter-in-law status." Sharing a chuckle feels almost irreverent, but also deeply necessary.

"Would it be all right if I have a french fry?" Erick holds both of his hands in the air as though he's the victim of a Wild West holdup.

"I'll allow it." Making a magnanimous gesture toward the platter, I smile and nod.

He bows his head in gratitude and selects a single fry from the heap.

Just one more reason for me to love this man.

CHAPTER 29

My father and his new wife, Amaryllis, arranged a belated honeymoon gift for Erick and me. Had the thaw come as usual, we would've been taking this helicopter ride on our actual anniversary, April 2nd. Instead, with things running late, we find ourselves high above Pin Cherry Harbor and our gorgeous great lake in May!

But this beats a Polish funeral procession any day of the week.

"Look! There's Bell, Book & Candle, and Myrtle's Diner! This is so cool. Where are we going? Did my dad tell you?"

As we fly over Fish Hawk Island, I wave down at Pin Cherry's most fancy dining establishment, Chez Osprey. Nimkii is likely in the kitchen giving the whole place a spring cleaning, despite his injured leg, but I wave anyway. He mentioned how he hopes to be open next weekend. Not with all this ice . . .

On the back side of the island, after we pass the lighthouse, the helicopter descends.

Erick is grinning from ear to ear.

"You know! You know where we're going. Tell me!" Unfortunately, Silas taught Erick the trick of filling his mind with the image of a snow princess when they were all working together to hide the elaborate marriage proposal from my detection. Right now, my husband is giving me nothing but *princess*.

Crossing my arms and pretending to have a pout buys me nothing. Pressing my face against the glass, I catch sight of the strange but sturdy-looking boat below. "Are we landing? On that weird boat?"

He can withhold his excitement no longer and a word slips by the snow princess.

"Icebreaker! We're landing on an icebreaker?"

Erick squeezes my hand and smiles like a kid on his way to see Santa Claus. "Your dad really has the connections, Moon. He and Amaryllis arranged for us to break the ice — literally."

"Seriously? We get to, like, unlock the harbor?"

"Yeah. Your dad said this ocean transport company he signed a deal with has huge pull. They made one phone call, and it was taken care of. Once they bust through and clear the shipping lane, they'll drop us at the marina. Odell said he'd pick us up."

"Odell knows, too? Man, Silas is gonna pull my psychic card. I didn't have a clue."

He puts a hand on my knee and squeezes. "You had a lot on your plate. Tug McAllister was trying to kill me. Artemis Ward was trying to kill you — and probably Silas. Plus, Pyewacket may or may not be some kind of god turned cat. I'd say it was a pretty full couple of weeks."

"Right?" I shake my head in disbelief. "I still don't know what's going on with Pyewacket. He's truly amazing. Grams says she won him in an 'off the books' Scrabble game, but I don't think that the exotic animal dealer had any idea what he had on his hands. If you ask me, Pyewacket orchestrated the entire thing. The supposed capture, the Scrabble game, and even my grandmother's triumph."

Erick bites his bottom lip. "Something to think about. I'll definitely be checking our stock of Fruit Puffs on a daily basis."

We share a chuckle as the pilot calls over his shoulder. "About to set down on the cutter. Could be a little bumpy, but nothing I haven't handled before."

My husband reaches out and holds my hand.

My heart swells. This guy . . . This amazing, brave, handsome man picked me. I mean, technically, I picked him and never took my finger off the trigger, but this version of the story has more romance. Right?

The skids hit the landing pad with a thud and skip twice.

I gasp, and possibly a muffled scream escapes despite my efforts to clamp my jaw.

Erick squeezes my hand. "We'll be fine."

The pilot shouts above the rotors, "Jump out. I can't shut her down in this weather. It's not safe."

Now he tells us! Erick unbuckles himself, then me, cranks the handle and we're out of the copter before I have time to wonder how the buckles work. He pulls me low, and we crouch and run toward a man with a thick blond beard who's waving to us.

The helicopter immediately takes off. As the sound dies down, the man welcomes us. "Good to see you both. I'm Captain Stubing. You're welcome to join me inside, or you can stand on the bow. It's going to be extremely bumpy, but there are locking straps and harnesses to secure yourselves with if you choose the outdoor option."

My voice seems to vanish, and my throat is instantly dry.

Erick, Mr. Ever-Calm, replies, "We'll join you

inside. We better get the lay of the land before we make any crazy plans."

The captain chuckles and leads the way back to the helm.

Powerful engines roar to life, and the boat lurches forward.

The captain explains, "We use the engines to force our reinforced hull onto the ice, and the weight of the vessel causes us to break through — creating chunks where there used to be a solid sheet. By increasing the surface area, the ice will melt more quickly. Some of the guys say all the vibration and shifting is like living in an endless earthquake." He chuckles and gives instructions to a crew member.

The creaking, scraping, and crunching is terrifying.

My dad really knows how to make a girl feel special. I thought first anniversaries were paper? I certainly hope the hull of this vessel is made from sturdier stuff.

The captain explains the value of his ship's service as the vessel lurches ahead. "We've got a couple of icebreakers out here today to open the harbor. We see millions of tons of freight come through here, and even a delay of a week or two can have a serious impact on the shipper as well as the factory waiting for raw materials. We'll likely have to make one or two more passes this week, but fore-casted temperatures are on a steady rise from here on out, you know." He pauses to answer a crew question, then changes tack. "I understand your father's in shipping?"

"My father is the owner of Midwest Union Railway. Used to be my Grandpa Cal's."

Captain Stubing's weathered face darkens. "That was bad business. Cal was a good man. I'm sorry for your loss."

It's odd. I never met Cal Duncan, and only saw him in death. When I later discovered that he wasn't my biological grandfather, my emotions surrounding his untimely death seemed to shift. It was sad, but didn't affect me directly. I mean, the fact that Erick arrested me for his murder would've affected me directly, but I fixed that. Right?

"She does that sometimes, Captain Stubing. She'll be with us in a minute."

The captain smiles. "My wife is the same way. She's got a hundred things racing through her head at any given moment. The fact that she can drive home from the grocery store without doing herself great bodily harm is something I'm grateful for daily."

He and Erick share quite a chuckle at my expense, but I'm a big girl and I let it go.

"Wait? That's your real name? You're not doing some kind of *Love Boat* joke?"

He grins. "I know. I probably should've changed my name the moment I chose my career path. The amount of flak I took for it in the Navy . . . Don't get me started."

"Sorry. I have a weird name, too. Mizithra. Named after a Greek cheese. I feel you, Captain."

Stubing smiles warmly. "Now that sounds like a story."

I give him the Spark Notes version, and he smiles. "Glad to hear you and your father found each other. As many days as I spend out here on the water, family is very important to me. Unless there's a life-threatening emergency, I'm always home for birthdays, anniversaries, and Christmas."

"What about Halloween?"

This brings a full-on belly laugh from the captain. "I'm definitely gonna have to introduce you to my wife. She talked me into doing a haunted cruise for Halloween every year. She decorates our private vessel so effectively, even I wonder if the boat wasn't simply dragged from the bottom of the lake earlier that morning. Folks pay top dollar to ride around on the haunted ship, eat creepy food, and dance until midnight. If you guys aren't doing anything in October, give me a call."

My eyes are glistening with anticipation, and I

squeeze Erick's arm. "I'm pretty sure you'll be hearing from us, Captain."

After nearly an hour of ice breaking, Erick convinces me to try the deck. The captain slows forward progress while we get ourselves strapped in.

Although I've been informed we're in the middle of the thaw, the temperatures amidst the icy winds swirling over the lake make this outdoor experience less than ideal.

After less than fifteen minutes, my pink cheeks, icy eyelashes, and sore neck have had enough.

Erick signals the captain. We unhook and head back inside.

"When the wind chill drops us below freezing, my crew is limited to ten-minute shifts out there. You head down to the galley, Harper. There's always hot chocolate and peppermint cookies. My wife picks them up from a bakery in Silver Shoals."

The reference to the scene of Tug McAllister's brutal actions causes a quickening of Erick's heartbeat.

Captain Stubing places a hand on Erick's shoulder. "Hey, I heard you guys caught those convicts and got them back to Clearwater. I know everyone up north will be grateful. When we lost Todd and Carry Engen in that terrible double homicide in Silver Shoals, it was heartbreaking for the whole community."

My humble husband nods his head and looks at the deck. "Just doing my job."

I want to remind him that he's no longer sheriff, and it's not his job to protect the community, but somewhere deep inside, I know he's right. And I know how important it is to him to be useful.

No matter what happens with our detective agency, I'll always be grateful that Erick and I can serve our community together. This is an orphan's dream. A husband. A stable home. Being surrounded by family and friends who truly care.

A loud crash and screech interrupt my reverie. The captain announces, "The harbor is open! Let me get you folks to the marina, and I'll let my wife know we have two confirmed for the Davey Jones' Haunted Cruise.

"Thank you, Captain Stubing." I try not to snicker, but you know me . . .

Erick leads me to the deck, and the icy wind is somewhat cut as we stand on the lee side of the bridge.

"Let's get down to the galley and warm up with some of that hot chocolate." My teeth chatter, and I rub my arms in an attempt to get the blood moving.

In place of an answer, my husband drops onto one knee and opens a small box — with its own LED light.

"That's gorgeous!" As I gaze down at the aurora

borealis dancing through the fire opal in its rose gold setting, my heart swells with love. "How did you know?"

His defenses drop, and I get a big psychic hit of Grams and him planning this elaborate "new ring" event.

He rises, removes my mitten, and slips the ring on my finger. "Perfect fit."

Straining to reach my tiptoes in snow boots, I bring my lips as close to his pouty mouth as possible. "Just like you and me, Harper. Just like you and me.

His lips are on mine as a foghorn echoes across the harbor.

Happy belated anniversary to us!

End of Book 5

But, the mysteries continue...
Curl up with the next book in the Harper and
Moon Investigations series!

A NOTE FROM TRIXIE

That Silas Willoughby is something else, but Pyewacket stole the show (*for me*)! Thank you for joining Mitzy and Erick on their new adventures in **Harper and Moon Investigations**. As always, I'll keep writing them if you keep reading . . .

The best part of "living" in Pin Cherry Harbor continues to be feedback from my early readers. Thank you to my alpha readers/cheerleaders, Angel, Claire, and Erin. HUGE thanks to my fantastic beta readers who always give me actionable and honest feedback: Veronica McIntyre and Nadine Peterse-Vrijhof. And big "small town" hugs to the world's best ARC Team – Trixie's Mystery ARC Detectives!

My creative editor Philip Newey provided important notes on plot holes. Many thanks to him! I enjoy getting his feedback as I improve each case. I'd also like to give a shout out to Roxx at Proof Perfect for the insightful proofing! Any remaining errors are my own.

Big thanks to Chad for reminding me that Mitzy needed a new ring! Also, thank you to Morgan for coming up with the "three convicts" angle.

FUN FACT: I've actually placed a lawn chair in a snowbank to "sun tan" during an almost-Canada-spring!

My favorite line from this case: "Safety was within my grasp, but I chose to risk it all in search of more comfortable clothes." ~Mitzy

I'm currently grieving a massive loss in my personal life and hope to write book six in the **Harper and Moon Investigations** series, *Wheels and Dirty Deals,* soon. All your *Mitzy Moon Mysteries* series favorites will continue on — but there will definitely be a murder!

Thank you for continuing to hang out with us.

Trixie Silvertale (April 2024)

Harper and Moon Investigations No. 6

A cryptic murder. A complete lack of suspects. Can our psychic sleuth find a lead or is she spinning her wheels?

Mitzy Moon is brimming with excitement. Planning an anniversary surprise, she's working overtime to hide the details of a luxurious European vacation from her husband. But before she can book a single ticket, a shockingly suspicious murder lands in her lap.

With only a flimsy lead, Mitzy heads under-cover into the local roller derby league. And though she rallies her entitled feline and meddling Ghost-ma to help hunt down clues, she fears if she can't break out of the pack, this bout will turn deadly.

Can Mitzy find the killer, or will this be her final lap around the track?

Wheels and Dirty Deals is the sixth book in the hilarious paranormal cozy mystery series, Harper and Moon Investigations, a spinoff from the popular Mitzy Moon Mysteries. If you like snarky heroines, supernatural intrigue, and a dash of romance, then you'll love Trixie Silvertale's twisty mystery.

Buy Wheels and Dirty Deals to put the guilty in the penalty box today!

Grab yours!
https://readerlinks.com/l/5211932

Scan this QR Code with the camera on your phone. You'll be taken right to the next Harper and Moon Investigations case.

Once you're in the Club, you'll also be the first to receive

updates from Pin Cherry Harbor and access to giveaways, new release announcements, short stories, behind-the-scenes secrets, and much more!

Scan this QR Code with the camera on your phone. You'll be taken right to the page to join the Club and get your FREE Novella!

THANK YOU!

Trying out a new book is always a risk and I'm thankful that you rolled the dice with Mitzy Moon. If you loved the book, the sweetest thing you can do (*even sweeter than pin cherry pie à la mode*) is to leave a review so that other readers will take a chance on Mitzy, Erick, and the gang.

Don't feel you have to write a book report. A brief comment like, "Can't wait to read the next book in this series!" will potential readers make their choice.

★★★★★
Leave a quick review HERE

https://readerlinks.com/l/3895372
★★★★★
Thank you, and I'll see you in Pin Cherry Harbor!

Heists and Poltergeists: Paranormal Cozy Mystery

Blades and Bridesmaids: Paranormal Cozy Mystery

Scones and Tombstones: Paranormal Cozy Mystery

Vandals and Yule Scandals: Paranormal Cozy Mystery

Harper and Moon Investigations

Ropes and Last Hopes: Paranormal Cozy Mystery

Bells and Bombshells: Paranormal Cozy Mystery

Rodeo Clowns and Shakedowns: Paranormal Cozy Mystery

Stiffs and Petroglyphs: Paranormal Cozy Mystery

Fatal Wines and Valentines: Paranormal Cozy Mystery

April Curses and May Hearses: Paranormal Cozy Mystery

Wheels and Dirty Deals: Paranormal Cozy Mystery

Scripts and Empty Crypts: Paranormal Cozy Mystery

Christmas Catastrophe Mysteries

Peppermint Cookie Murder: Paranormal Cozy Mystery

Apple Dumpling Murder: Paranormal Cozy Mystery

Linzer Cookie Murder: Paranormal Cozy Mystery

Chocolate Crinkle Cookie Murder: Paranormal Cozy Mystery

...more to come!

MAGICAL RENAISSANCE FAIRE MYSTERIES

Explore the world of Coriander the Conjurer. A fortune-telling fairy with a heart of gold!

Book 1:

All Swell That Ends Spell – A dubious festival. A fatal swim. Can this fortune-telling fairy herald the true killer?

Book 2:

Fairy Wives of Windsor – A jolly Faire. A shocking murder. Can this furtive fairy outsmart the killer?

Book 3:

Double Double Royal Trouble – When a treat-peddling witch is found dead, will this cursed faire crumble?

Join Sydney Coleman and her unruly ghosts, as they solve mysteries in a truly haunted mansion!

Book 1: **Moonlight and Mischief** – She's desperate for a fresh start, but is a mansion on sale too good to be true?

Book 2: **Moonlight and Magic** – A haunted Halloween tour seem like the perfect plan, until there's murder...

Book 3: ***Moonlight and Mayhem*** – An unwelcome visitor. A surprising past. Will her fire sale end in smoke?

ABOUT THE AUTHOR

USA TODAY Bestselling author Trixie Silvertale grew up reading an endless supply of Lilian Jackson Braun, Hardy Boys, and Nancy Drew novels. She loves the amateur sleuths in cozy mysteries and obsesses about all things paranormal. Those two passions unite in her Harper and Moon Investigations, and she's thrilled to write them and share them with you.

When she's not consumed by writing, she bakes to fuel her creative engine and pulls weeds in her herb garden to clear her head (*and sometimes she pulls out her hair, but mostly weeds*).

Greetings are welcome:
trixie@trixiesilvertale.com

BB bookbub.com/authors/trixie-silvertale

f facebook.com/TrixieSilvertale

instagram.com/trixiesilvertale